Breathe Again

Adrienne Thompson

Pink Cashmere Publishing, LLC
Arkansas, USA

Copyright © 2017 by Adrienne Thompson

Cover art by AA Thompson (thompson9699@gmail.com)

All rights reserved. This book or any portion thereof may not be reproduced or used in any manner whatsoever without the express written permission of the publisher except for the use of brief quotations in a book review.

This is a work of fiction. Names, characters, businesses, places, events and incidents are either the products of the author's imagination or used in a fictitious manner. Any resemblance to actual persons, living or dead, or actual events is purely coincidental.

Printed in the United States of America

First Printing 2017

Pink Cashmere Publishing, LLC
pinkcashmerepub@gmail.com
http://pinkcashmerepublishing.webs.com/

A special thank you to Letrece Harris for sharing your insight on being an NFL wife. I truly appreciate you taking the time to help me. Any errors are mine and not hers.

Thanks so much to the readers who continue to purchase and read my work. I hope you enjoy *Breathe Again* as much as I enjoyed writing it.

"Be kind and compassionate to one another, forgiving each other, just as in Christ God forgave you." - *Ephesians 4:32 (NIV)*

"It's one of the greatest gifts you can give yourself, to forgive. Forgive everybody." - *Maya Angelou*

Soundtrack

"Help" *Erica Campbell featuring Lecrae*
"In the Sanctuary" *Kurt Carr Singers*
"Superstar" *Tyrone Tribbett*
"Whatcha Lookin' 4" *Kirk Franklin & The Family*
"I Feel Your Spirit" *Hezekiah Walker*
"Faith to Believe" *Sheri Jones Moffett*
"Take Care Of You" *Fred Hammond*
"Here For You" *Travis Greene*
"Heart to Yours" *Michelle Williams*
"When Sunday Comes" *Daryl Coley*
"Stranger" *Donald Lawrence*
"Higher" *William Murphy*
"The Way You See Me" *James Fortune & Fiya*
"It's Alright, it's OK" *Shirley Caesar featuring Anthony Hamilton*
"Blessings" *Laura Story*
"Beauty For Ashes" *Tye Tribbett*
"Livin'" *The Clark Sisters*
"Love" *God's Property*
"Fly Like a Bird" *Mariah Carey*
"Good and Bad" *J Moss*
"Never Let Go" *Kim Burrell*
"Try" *DeWayne Woods*
"Supposed To Be" *BeBe & CeCe Winans*
"Stand" *Donnie McClurkin*
"Break Every Chain" *Tasha Cobbs*
"Addictive Love" *BeBe & CeCe Winans*

one
"Help"

"You'll do it, won't you?"

I groaned softly. "But I'm working with the hospitality committee. You want me to meet and greet this man and introduce him, too?"

"It's a special request from the pastor. He says you have the voice for it," Sister Green reiterated.

I sighed and dropped into my recliner, grabbed my laptop. The pastor, huh? What was I supposed to do? Refuse the pastor? "All right. What's his name again? I guess I need to do some research on him, get his background information."

"You don't have to worry about that. You know he's Mother Millie's grandson. She said her daughter already wrote the introduction. I'll get it to you."

Well, that was a relief. "Okay." I rubbed my forehead. "Um, I need to go, Sister Green. Talk to you later."

"Okay, sugar. Be blessed."

"You, too."

I ended the call and dialed my brother's number. He answered with, "Hey, baby sis!"

"Don't you 'baby sis' me! Felton, you sicced Sister Green on me?"

He chuckled. "Sicced? That's a bit dramatic, isn't it?"

"You couldn't ask me yourself?"

"I knew you'd say no."

"How do you know I didn't tell *her* no?"

"Because I know you. Once she told you I requested it, you *had* to accept. You know as well as I do she would've fired up the gossip mill if you refused to do this for me: 'Pastor and his sister done fell out, girl. Mm-hmm. They sho' have.'"

I couldn't help but giggle at his spot-on impression of her. She was as messy as she claimed to be holy. "You need to quit. What kind of pastor says stuff like that?"

"A truthful one."

"Felt, I already have a lot on my plate, and don't we usually let one of the kids introduce the Youth Day speaker?"

"You *are* one of the kids, baby sis."

"Felt, I'm twenty-seven years old."

"I know…It was Spring's idea. She thinks you need to be seen more."

I rolled my eyes. My dear, sweet sister-in-law was forever trying to "help" me find a man. I was sure this was her latest attempt along those lines. "She needs to stop."

"She loves you."

"I love her, too, and she *still* needs to stop. What does she think I'ma do? Hook up with the speaker? An NFL player?"

"No, she just wants to get you in front of the church."

"Oh, she wants one of the kids' married fathers to see me?"

"There'll be single men there, too, I'm sure."

"You're sure?" I sighed. "I'ma do it, but you need to tell your First Lady to stop."

"Like she's gonna listen to me..."

I laughed. "You do have a point. Look, I gotta get ready for work. See you Sunday."

"All right, sis."

I hung up, threw on my uniform, and headed out the door.

***

I knocked, waited a couple of minutes, then used my key to let myself into the house. "Daddy?" I called into the darkness. It was a little after 11:00 PM, and I was sure he was already in bed, but I needed to check on him. Somebody had to.

I navigated my way through the living room to the kitchen where I opened the refrigerator, shedding some light, and then turned and eyed the sink to find it full of dishes. I shook my head as I placed the greasy sack of ribs on a shelf next to a six-pack of beer and closed the refrigerator door. Leaving the kitchen, I tiptoed to the bedroom, finding it easy to make the familiar trip in the blackness. Just as I expected, Daddy was fast asleep, wearing a dingy t-shirt and old khakis as he lay on top of the neatly-made bed, an empty beer bottle lying next to him like a beloved teddy bear. I grabbed a blanket from a kitchen chair he kept in the corner of the bedroom and covered him up. He stirred a bit when I kissed his cheek. Then I left, deciding that yet another of his helpers would have to be fired.

two

"In the Sanctuary"

I entered the pastor's study, and before I could utter a word, my sister-in-law hopped up from her seat in front of my brother's desk and snatched me into a hug, then whispered, "The whole introduction thing was Felton's idea," in my ear.

I fought not to roll my eyes. One of them was lying, and if it was Spring, she was lying in the church house, of all places. Anything to keep me from going off on her, I suppose. I stepped out of the hug and ran my hands over the front of my navy-blue dress. "I'm not in here about that." I turned my attention to my older brother who looked distinguished and handsome as always in his black suit. He reminded me so much of our father. Well, he reminded me of who Daddy used to be.

"Felton," I said, "I'm here about that girl you hired to help Daddy."

He laid his hands on his Bible. "Can it wait until later? I was just about to call the deacons in and pray over this morning's service."

"It'll only take a second. I've got work after service. Or I can just slide into the pulpit and discuss it with you during one of the choir's selections."

He sighed. "What's going on?"

"We need to find someone else. I dropped by to check on Daddy the other evening and he had a sink full of dishes and a refrigerator full of beer. Now we both know Daddy didn't go to the store and buy that beer himself."

"We don't know that Asha did, either. Daddy has friends," Felton said.

"Look, the only reason I moved out is because you kept telling me I needed to be on my own and stop hovering over him. I see now that was a mistake. That girl you hired bought that beer. Daddy's friends know better."

"Okay, okay...I'll deal with it."

I smirked. "You better."

I left, still fuming. Felton always took things too lightly when it came to Daddy. If it wasn't for me, there was no telling what condition our father would be in. And on top of being upset about my father, I was in no mood to be at church and was in even less of a mood to introduce Mother Millie's football star, or wannabe star, grandson. Shoot, I didn't even like football. Never watched it, because my father didn't like football. He was a boxing fan. Ask me about Ali, Frazier, Tyson, or Mayweather, and I got you. But football? Nope.

At least they took the hospitality duties from me after I got roped into doing this intro. Someone else would have to meet and greet our guests.

I entered the sanctuary and made my way to a seat on a pew near the podium that sat on the floor, to the left of the pulpit, and waited for service to begin.

***

When my name was announced, I was in a much brighter mood. The youth choir was in rare form that day, and the Holy Spirit was definitely in the house. I was so full, I nearly floated to the podium.

I read the introduction just as it was given to me, just as I had rehearsed it twice at home. Rattled off the awards and achievements that I didn't fully understand, but they seemed to hold more weight as I shared them with the congregation. Even *I* was impressed that he'd completed his accounting degree after being drafted into the NFL and felt a little sheepish about not bothering to meet him before service. I had no idea what this impressive-on-paper man looked like, but I would find out shortly.

I ended the introduction with: "Now, brothers, sisters, and youth, I introduce to some and present to others, NFL superstar…Malachi Douglass!!"

The church erupted in applause as I reclaimed my seat, and a brother I hadn't noticed rose from the center of the church and approached the podium. A tall, muscular, chocolate brother wearing a tailored charcoal gray suit, white shirt, and black tie. Neat beard, thick hair cropped close to his head, bright smile. My insides churned. I should've looked this man up on the Internet so I would've been better prepared, because as it was, all I could do was sit there and stare at him open-mouthed. The man was fine, super fine, *super-duper* fine. Real, real, *real* fine. And it wasn't like I'd never seen a fine man before, but this man was downright…sexy.

I fiddled with the hem of my dress as he said something I was too frazzled to make out. The congregation laughed. So did I, though I didn't know why.

I heard him say, "I'd like to thank the beautiful young lady for the overly-flattering introduction," and I nearly melted. He'd called me beautiful. I pinched my thigh through the fabric of my dress. Told myself to come back to the world. He was saying that because it was a nice thing to say. Not that I was refuting the beautiful part. I knew I looked nice. I always tried to look my best for church. But this man was tall, handsome, and famous. He looked to be the type who'd prefer a more petite type of woman—a trophy wife. I certainly wasn't that. Not that I was humongous or anything, but I was definitely on the thicker side. But God and all His heavenly hosts knew he was my type—fine!

He continued to speak, but I didn't hear a word of it. My mouth was dry and my face was flushed and I needed a fan, because I was sure my armpits were growing moist. His voice was deep and smooth and hypnotic. Everything about him absolutely appealed to me. And that disturbed me. I couldn't remember the last time a man affected me like that. When was the last time just seeing a man and hearing him talk made me feel so…well, so much like a woman?

A burst of applause pulled me from my semi-conscious state, and I watched him walk back to his seat with a swagger akin to that of President Obama's. He graciously shook hands with the people seated close to him. Then he looked in my direction and nodded with that beautiful smile still on his face. I dropped my eyes, felt my heart knock against my rib cage, and wrung my hands in my lap. I would be so glad when service was over. I felt like a wiggly, wobbly mound of Jell-O sitting there all sweaty and weak.

I made my escape during offering, dropped my envelope in the basket at the altar and walked right out of one of the side doors, down the hall, through the foyer, and out the front doors, making quick steps to my old Nissan Maxima. I rested my head on the steering wheel before starting the car and heading home to get ready for work.

three
"Superstar"

Brown Boy's Barbecue was owned and operated by my uncle, Felix Brown Jr., my father's oldest brother, and had been for as long as I could remember. As a child, we would go to Brown Boy's every Sunday after church for dinner. That had ended when my mother left. I wasn't sure when my father last visited there, but it'd probably been at least ten years since he stepped foot in the tiny, stand-alone restaurant that could boast of having once been both a donut shop and a nightclub at different points in time. It had housed Brown Boy's for the past fifteen years, since a fire destroyed the original restaurant's building across town.

My uncle opened his first restaurant over thirty years ago. Now it was a fixture in our small town and was at the top of many people's list of favorite places to eat. Ask my uncle, and he'd say it was because of my late grandfather's vinegar-based barbecue sauce, a recipe my uncle vowed would only be shared during the reading of his will.

I'd been working there for nearly eleven years, since the week after my sixteenth birthday, and I can honestly say I loved it, but I was still so off-balance from the doggone football player's smile and body and...*everything*, I asked Anika to switch positions with me. She happily agreed to wait tables, knowing the tips would be good on a Sunday, our busiest day. I took her post in the back where I helped my ever-hands-on uncle fill the orders.

I was deep in the trenches, scooping tangy coleslaw into Styrofoam pint containers, when Anika peeped in the kitchen and called my name.

"Yeah?" I said, without looking up.

"Your brother's here, and he's asking for you."

I released a tiny sigh and removed the vinyl gloves from my hands, followed Anika out the door, and upon seeing my brother and his table mates, ducked back into the kitchen, dragging Anika with me.

She jerked away from me. "Girl, what's wrong with you, grabbing me like that? I think you bruised my arm!"

"Tell my brother I'm not here," I whispered.

"I already told him you *are* here. And why are we whispering?"

"Tell him you made a mistake."

"I ain't lying to no preacher, Maria! Now, come on!"

"Something wrong, niece?" Uncle Felix asked.

"Um..." I snatched my apron off and shook my head. "No, sir. Felton Jr. is out there asking for me. Probably wants me to work his table."

"You don't want to?"

"Not really."

"Then you shouldn't be the best. Go on out there." He started hacking at a slab of ribs before I could respond.

I took a deep breath, left the kitchen, and approached Felton's table.

"Hey, baby sis!"

I nodded, swung my eyes from my brother to his co-conspiring wife, and then to *him*, sitting there with an empty lap I could see myself sitting on if I ever developed a bold bone in my body. He smiled at me, and I had to fight the desire to run out the door and onto the parking lot.

"Hi," he said.

I stared at him for a minute or so and then returned my attention to my brother, said, "What are y'all having?" I wasn't trying to be rude. I was just afraid if I responded to Malachi Douglass, I would sound like some lunatic, because I couldn't think of one single coherent word to say to him.

Felton cleared his throat and shot a glance at his wife before saying, "Give us the Big Brown and a pitcher of sweet tea. I want to make sure Mr. Douglass here gets a good taste of our town *and* our family's barbecue."

"Can't wait," Malachi said. His words were for my brother, but his eyes were on me.

I nodded and scurried back to the kitchen.

"Niece, what is going on with you?" Uncle Felix asked, still holding that meat cleaver, his trusty apron splattered with grease.

I looked up at the older version of my father and forced a smile. "Nothing. Why do you ask?"

"Because you standing there by that door looking like you just saw a ghost."

"It's…Felton Jr. has that football player at the table with him."

He placed the cleaver on the counter, wiped his hands on his apron.

He never wore gloves. "What football player?" he asked.

"The one who spoke at church today."

"I ain't set foot inside a church in twenty years, and you know it."

"I keep inviting you."

"What football player? What's his name? Who he play for?"

I threw up my hands. "Malachi something. I forget who he plays for…"

The next thing I knew, Uncle Felix had swept past me, almost knocking me down on his way out the door. I stood there for ten minutes before peeping out the door to see he'd joined Felton and Spring and Malachi at the table. There was a small crowd of customers standing around them, hanging on Malachi's every word. I shook my head as I went about the task of gathering the food for their order.

I was almost done when Anika stuck her head in the door. "You need some help?"

"No, I got it."

"Naw, girl. Let me help you."

I eyed her. Anika was tall and lanky and was currently sporting a very curly wig and bright red lipstick. She hadn't been wearing lipstick before. "You finally noticed the guy at my brother's table, huh?"

"Oh, I noticed him when he walked in the door. Can't miss a man that sexy. I just didn't know who he was or that he was rich."

"You got a man."

"That man at your brother's table is making me rethink some things."

"You are not dumping Oren for nobody. You love him too much."

"Humph."

Anika took the huge platter of food while I carried the plates and rolled silverware, all of which I nearly dropped when I opened the door to find Malachi standing on the other side.

His eyes swept over me, and he smiled. "Maria?"

For a second, I seriously wondered if that was really my name, but managed to give him a nod, still afraid to speak.

"Um, can you show me where the restroom is?"

Before I could answer, Uncle Felix came up behind Malachi, rested a heavy hand on his shoulder, and said, "Show him to the executive restroom, niece," with a wink.

As I fixed my mouth to protest, he emptied my hands of their burden and left me standing there with my heart throbbing like the beat of a RuPaul song.

We stood there for a good thirty seconds before I turned, and said, "Sure, follow me." I gave myself a mental high-five for almost sounding normal.

"Thank you," he said, as he followed me through the kitchen to the tiny, but clean, employee restroom.

"Um, here it is."

He nodded slightly and eased past me. "Will you wait for me? I might get lost on my way back."

I frowned slightly. "Are you serious?" It was a straight path through the kitchen to the dining room.

He stared down at my five-foot, four-inch frame and smiled. "I'm very serious."

The depth of his voice seeped into me, making me feel anxious. All I could do was nod in agreement and then sit in a corner of the kitchen and try to catch my breath.

I heard him emerge from the bathroom, and he actually looked relieved when he saw me waiting in the kitchen for him. After leading him back to his table, I spent the next hour wading through a crowd of his admirers, trying to serve his table. I was so glad when he left.

four

"Whatcha Lookin' 4"

"I heard this place was packed yesterday," Carl Jr., my cousin and Uncle Felix's grandson, said as I unlocked the front door to the restaurant.

"Yeah, we were crazy busy," I replied.

"And I heard Malachi was here."

I gave him a sideways glance as we both entered the kitchen. "You say his name like you know him or something."

"Come on, cuz. Who *don't* know Malachi? He's one of the baddest receivers in the NFL! Got a bunch of endorsement deals, too. Malachi is the man!"

I shrugged. "I don't know a thing about him. I don't do football."

"Man, I wish I'd been here. I would've had him sign my jersey. That's one bad dude!"

I didn't know how bad of a dude he was, but I did know he dominated my dreams all night long, had me sweaty and exhausted by the time I crawled out of bed that morning. "Well, you better be a bad dude at prepping this food. You're in the kitchen today. I'm out front," I said. We always ran a light crew on Monday—our slowest day of the week.

He gave me a salute. "Got it, boss lady."

I rolled my eyes and continued preparing to open the restaurant.

After a small lunchtime rush, I planted my butt on the stool behind the counter and pulled out my phone. My intention was to mindlessly scroll through my Twitter and Facebook feeds, but I found myself opening the Safari app and searching the name Malachi Douglass. On his Wikipedia page, I saw most of the stuff I'd read in his introduction with a few more detailed stats about his high school and college careers added. He was twenty-six, six-foot-one, youngest son of Tina Douglass. No father listed.

I heard the bell over the door ring, but kept my eyes on the phone, figuring I'd give whoever it was a minute or so to peruse the menu that hung above the counter.

Malachi Douglass resides in Dallas, where he grew up—

"Excuse me."

That voice.

I set my phone on the counter and slowly lifted my eyes. He looked just as good in a t-shirt and jeans as he had in that expensive suit the day before. "Um, hi," I mumbled. "Welcome to Brown Boy's."

He smiled. "Hi, yourself."

Some woman I wasn't familiar with used my mouth to say, "Back so soon?"

He slid his hands into the pockets of his jeans and lifted his shoulders a bit. "What can I say? I like good food, especially good barbecue."

The same woman made me lean across the counter and smile. "Well, I'm glad you enjoyed it. You dining in or getting something to go?"

He glanced around the empty dining room. "I think I'll dine in."

"Cool, pick a table. I'll be over to take your order in a moment."

He eyed me a second or two, and replied with, "I'll look forward to it, Maria."

My lips involuntarily curved into another smile as I watched him walk away, taking note of how his jeans fit his behind. He was truly a sexy man, and I almost thought he was flirting with me. I must've been losing my mind.

I spun around to find Carl Jr. standing behind me with his mouth hung open. Nudging him, I said, "Why don't you take him a menu and a cup of water for me?"

His eyes darted to me and back to Malachi's table. "For real?"

"Yeah, for real. But close your mouth first."

Carl Jr. nervously grabbed a paper menu and left. He had to come back for the water. I gave him a few minutes with his hero before approaching the table to take Malachi's order. Carl Jr. promptly hopped up from his seat, autographed menu in hand, and bounced back to his post in the kitchen.

"You ready to order, Mr. Douglass?" I asked.

"Malachi."

"Okay…um, Malachi. You ready to order?"

"Yeah, let me get two rib sandwich meals. Two cups of sweet tea."

"Two?"

"Two. I'm expecting someone."

"Oh...sides?"

"Baked beans and potato salad."

"Great, let me get that right out to you."

My smile had disappeared when I left his table. So he was meeting someone, but who? Probably one of the desperate single women from my church. Or better yet, one of those heifers who were hawking his and my brother's table the day before. Whatever. There was no sense in me getting all in my feelings about it. It wasn't like there was a chance of us getting together, and it might have been a guy he was meeting, anyway. Maybe it wasn't a date. At any rate, it wasn't my business or my concern.

When Carl Jr. slid the tray of Malachi's food through the window that connected the kitchen to the front counter, I said, "You take it to him."

With wide eyes, he said, "For real, cuz?"

I nodded.

He was as giddy as a five-year-old meeting SpongeBob instead of a twenty-year-old college student. I had reclaimed my seat at the counter when Carl Jr. returned, and said, "He's asking for you."

"Who?" I asked, as if there was anyone else in the nearly-empty restaurant.

"Malachi."

I released a sigh. "All right. I'll check on him in a second," I said, taking a moment to plaster a smile on my face before approaching him. "Hey, did you need something?"

He grinned up at me and nodded. "I need for you to join me."

"Huh?"

"I'd like for you to have lunch with me."

I frowned slightly. What kind of game was this? Had he been stood up, and was using me to pass the time? "I thought you were meeting someone."

"I am. I'm meeting *you*."

I shook my head. "I don't—"

"Look, Maria. I like you. So much so, that I called your brother and asked him if you'd be at work today. I also asked him what your favorite thing on the menu was."

My jaw dropped. "What? But you don't know me."

"I'd like to get to know you."

I searched my brain for something else to say, came up with, "Uh, aren't you leaving soon?"

"Next Sunday. Hanging out at my grandmother's until then."

"So we have lunch and you're hoping to do what? Sleep with my little country bumpkin, backwards, backwoods butt and then disappear, go back to your life like nothing happened?"

He looked a little bewildered. "Damn…uh, no. I ain't perfect, but I don't do stuff like that. I want to have lunch with you, talk to you, see you again before I leave, exchange phone numbers with you. I just wanna get to know you, Maria Brown. And I know you haven't eaten yet. Your brother also told me you usually skip lunch. So…have a seat."

I looked down into his deep chocolate eyes and felt my pulse quicken. "Um…I'm-I'm at work."

"Looks like business is slow right now. Sit with me." He stood from his seat, walked around, and pulled the other chair out for me.

Well, there wasn't any sense in me pretending I wasn't hungry. And now I was not only attracted to this man but intrigued by him. So I sat my wide butt down, said a silent grace, and dug in. "Thank you."

"No problem. This is something I can check off my bucket list."

"What? Eating barbecue in a hole in the wall in Arkansas?"

"Eating barbecue with the prettiest—" he flashed a smile, "—and sexiest woman I've ever met."

I smirked but wanted to grin. "Have we met? I don't remember us meeting."

He extended his hand across the table to me. "Hi, I'm Malachi Levi Douglass."

I took his huge, warm hand and swallowed hard when he squeezed mine. "I'm Maria Rose Brown."

"Maria Rose Brown. Hmmm, sounds like the answer to my prayers."

I hesitantly pulled my hand from his. "What have you been praying for exactly?"

"Love. *Real* love."

"How do you know I'm not already taken?"

He gave me a lopsided grin. "No ring, plus I asked—"

"My brother."

"Right."

"I'm gonna kill him," I muttered.

"Why? You don't want to get to know me? I can give you much more adequate information than Wikipedia."

I cringed. "You saw my phone…"

"Yep."

I sighed. "Okay, okay. So…I was-I *am* curious."

"Good. Because I'm *more* than curious when it comes to you."

I smiled. "Is that so?"

He leaned across the table and looked me in the eye. "Yes, it is. I can show you better than I can tell you…if you let me."

"Okay…show me."

five

"I Feel Your Spirit"

He showed up at the restaurant and had lunch with me the next two days. Even when things would get busy, he'd sit at his table and wait, kindly chat with the other patrons, and sign autographs. He was very humble and gracious from what I could tell, and all of that on top of being drop-dead gorgeous. I must admit, I was more than flattered that he was spending so much time trying to woo me.

I learned a lot about him—that he was the youngest of five children raised by a single mother. That he grew up in the projects and that his talent had saved his entire family from poverty. I told him I was the younger of two children and had lived here in Beckton, Arkansas, since the day I was born.

Three lunch dates later, I stood in front of the floor-to-ceiling mirror hanging on my bathroom door and held a dress up to my body for about the tenth time in as many minutes. Nothing looked right. Nothing was good enough, or at least nothing was good enough to be seen wearing in his presence. Why had I agreed to a date—an actual grown people's date? I hadn't been on a date in years. Since high school.

I plopped down on my bed and dialed my father's number. I hadn't been back to visit him, because I honestly didn't have the heart to see him like that again. I'd spent the better part of my life after my mother left cleaning him up, helping him to bed, throwing away empty beer cans and bottles, and it had taken a toll on me. I loved my father and wanted to respect him, but he made it hard. Sometimes I wanted to shake him and yell at him to move on, to let my mother go. But I knew it wasn't that easy. Nothing ever was.

"Hello?" His gravelly voice filled my ear.

"Hey, Daddy. Just calling to check on you. You okay?"

"I would be if you and Junior would stop firing my help. Asha was a nice girl."

So, Felton had followed through on my request. Good. "She shouldn't have been buying you beer. And she wasn't cleaning up."

"She did what I asked her to do."

"Well, if you want to keep your help, stop asking them to do things they don't need to be doing. You got a new helper?"

"Yeah, some old, uptight woman. Shoot, she won't even buy me a Coke."

"Since you're a diabetic, that's a good thing."

"You coming over tonight? Bring me some ribs."

"No, I'll have to come tomorrow. I have a date tonight." It was so weird hearing myself say that.

"A date?"

"Yes, a date. And I need to get ready. I'll talk to you later. Love you, Daddy."

"Love you, too."

**

He picked me up in a Range Rover, came to my door dressed in slacks and a dress shirt open just enough to give me a peek at his chest. I licked my lips when I opened the door and welcomed him into my house, a family home my paternal uncles had agreed to let me live in rent-free. "Hey," I said with a smile.

He watched me close my front door and eyed me for a moment, finally said, "You look beautiful. You're so beautiful, I could just stand here all night and stare at you."

"Thank you. You always know the right things to say, don't you?"

"No, I speak the truth. The truth is always the right thing to say."

I looked him up and down. "You're smooth, Mr. Douglass. You're smooth."

He shrugged. "I'm just me, Maria. That's all I can say."

"Hmm."

"You ready for me to show you a good time?"

"Yes."

I took his arm and let him escort me out of my house.

***

Two's was a tiny juke joint located in Malachi's hometown—Solid Rock, Arkansas, a little town with a population of three thousand people. To see him and know this was where he was born and had spent the early part of his life was mind-blowing.

Solid Rock was a once-thriving highway town that was one of the last stops before leaving Arkansas to enter Mississippi, depending on which route you took. The creation of the interstate many years earlier had made it little more than a couple of exit signs and had plunged the community into poverty. There were no jobs, few farms, and most people made ends meet via government assistance.

Two's was nothing more than a wooden shack hidden deep in the woods, accessible only by taking a narrow dirt road. I'd dressed up. So had Malachi, and my first thought when he parked on the worn grass behind the building was that we were terribly overdressed. But once we entered the tiny space, I saw that everyone had on their Sunday best. Two's wasn't much to look at inside or out, but it was clean and the atmosphere was dynamic.

Malachi led me to a table near the back, speaking to several people along the way. Once we'd taken our seats, I said, "You told me the other day you were only ten when you moved to Texas. How do you even know about this place?"

"It's my grandmother's."

My eyes widened. "Mother Millie owns this place?"

He chuckled and shook his head. "No, Ms. Two is more of a play grandmother, I guess. She helped my mother out a lot when I was little. Took a liking to me, kind of took me under her wing. She used to pay me to sweep up the place, wipe the tables. She was the one who gave my mom the money to move to Texas."

"She sounds like a wonderful person."

Before he could answer, a tall, heavy-set woman wearing an impossibly tight red dress, a red afro wig, and pink house slippers, hobbled over to us using a gold cane for support. She hovered over the table for a second and then burst into laughter. Malachi hopped up and nearly tackled the woman with a hug. "Ms. Two!!"

The lady dropped the cane and embraced Malachi. I could see tears coursing down her plump, rouged cheeks. "Boy, you went and got so famous, I thought you forgot about old Two!"

Malachi stepped out of her embrace and bent over to pick up her cane. "You know better than that. Haven't you been getting the checks?"

She took the cane and placed a hand on his cheek. She was almost as tall as him. "I been getting the money. Just so glad to see your pretty face. Just as pretty as you were when you were a baby. Talked to your mama the other day. She didn't tell me you were coming to town!"

He winked at her. "I told her not to."

She wiped her eyes. "You oughta be ashamed, doing old Two like that." She turned her attention to me. "Well, introduce me to your lady friend. Your mama didn't tell me about her, either."

Malachi reclaimed his seat, said, "Ms. Two, this is Maria Brown. I met her at my granny's church over in Beckton last Sunday."

"A church girl? Well, it's a pleasure to meet you, honey. I want you to enjoy yourself. You're in good hands, because I helped raise this one here myself. He knows how to treat a lady."

I smiled as I took the big, warm hand she offered. "Nice to meet you."

"Well, 'Chi, I need to get back to the kitchen. I'ma send you two some food right on out." She leaned over and kissed his forehead before hobbling away from our table.

"She seems really nice," I offered.

"Ms. Two is the best."

"Is Two her real name?"

He nodded. "Two Jones. There were ten kids in all, all named after the order of their birth, including twins named Six and Seven."

"Are you serious?"

"As a heart attack."

I laughed. "That sounds like something my daddy would say, not a twenty-something-year-old man."

"Folks always said I have an old soul."

"I believe it."

"What about you?"

"What about me?"

"What kind of soul do you have, Ms. Brown?"

"Hmm, I don't know? I hope a good one."

"You know what? We've had at least three face to face conversations, and I barely know anything about you. I've been running my mouth about myself."

I leaned back in my rickety metal and vinyl chair. "What do you want to know?"

"Anything."

"Well, you know I'm the baby of my family. My brother is five years older than me. You've already met him and his wife. Um, my father, Felton Sr., still lives in our family home…"

"What's he do for a living?"

"He doesn't work now, but he used to be a plumber and a preacher.

Never pastored a church, though. He was more of an evangelist."

"What about your mother?"

The hairs on my arms stood at attention, and the stuffy air in the place grew thin. I didn't answer immediately. I'd spent years trying not to sound odd when I spoke of her. I never succeeded. Finally, I said, "She's not in my life."

He nodded. "Same with my father."

I wanted to probe him about his father, but knew I wasn't ready to reciprocate if he had questions about my mother. So, I just dropped my eyes.

"What do you like to do? For fun?"

"Um, I used to sew a lot. I made most of my own clothes back in high school. I was good at drawing and painting, too. I thought I'd be an artist one day."

"What's stopping you now?"

I looked up at him and quickly dropped my eyes again. His gaze was too intense for me. "I have responsibilities—my father's not well. And I basically run the restaurant. My uncle only comes in occasionally. And I spend a lot of time at the church…"

I looked up again. He was still staring at me but with less intensity. He looked like he wanted to say something then thought better of it. After a few moments of silence, a woman who strongly resembled Ms. Two approached our table carrying two heaping plates of food.

"Thank you, Gladys," Malachi said.

The woman nodded and hurried away, returning seconds later with silverware and two glasses of water.

I smiled and thanked her. She nodded and nearly whispered, "You welcome," before quickly leaving again.

"Gladys is Ms. Two's daughter. She's a bit shy," Malachi explained.

"Oh…okay."

I turned my attention to the plate, which held a pig's foot drenched in hot sauce, pinto beans virtually swimming in grease, mustard greens intermingled with ham hock meat, and a thick slice of cornbread. I'd never seen anything that looked so appetizing and unhealthy before in all my life! Okay, that's a lie. My mother, Rhonda, used to throw down like that nearly every Saturday. Saturdays were for my mama's soul food. Sundays were for Brown Boy's.

A faint smile appeared on my face at the memory. It was one of the few good memories of my mother that remained. "Wow, this looks good!" I said, as I forked up a pile of greens.

Malachi nodded, chewed for a few seconds, and said, "It tastes even better."

I dug in, and by the time we were both finished, I was so stuffed I felt a little uncomfortable.

Malachi chuckled. "You look like I feel."

I sighed and readjusted my butt on the seat. "Then you must feel like you're about to pop."

"Yep." Hopping up, he reached for my hand. "Come on. Let's dance this food off. I think I just gained twenty pounds."

I took his hand, stood with a soft grunt. "I gained forty."

The dancefloor was a scuffed-up piece of black and white, checkered linoleum no more than ten feet by ten feet. We barely fit with the other three or four couples already on the floor moving to a mid-tempo song.

I was poised and ready to do my signature dainty two-step when the song ended and a slow jam I vaguely recognized began to play. Like all of the other music that had been playing in the background the entire time we'd been there, it was old and bluesy, made many years before my time. I knew the melody, but the lyrics and title escaped me. Malachi, the old soul, hummed along with the song as he pulled my body close to his and began rocking us back and forth, rubbing his hands up and down my back. I leaned into him a bit, but didn't totally relax in his arms. Yes, he was handsome and kind and had basically shared his life story with me, but I still found it hard to totally let my guard down. I still didn't know him. Not really. And he definitely didn't know me. I wasn't sure if I wanted him to know me.

So I placed my hands on his shoulders and backed away a little, gazing up at his face. If I looked into his eyes, maybe he'd see what I couldn't tell him—that I was petrified of what he represented and what he could offer me, even more afraid of him disappointing me.

He looked down at me, continuing to rock us back and forth as he mouthed the words to the song.

"Who's singing this song?" I asked.

"Hmm, Major Harris. *Love Won't Let Me Wait*. One of my favorites." He pulled me closer. I didn't resist. "It's one of my mom's favorites, too."

I leaned into him and tried not to cry. Now I knew why it was familiar. Although she preferred Luther Vandross's version, that song was one of *my* mother's favorite songs, as well.

That song and the feelings it evoked ruined the rest of the night for me. There I sat across from a man most women would jump through hoops to spend time with, and all I could do was think of my mother and the things she'd done that had ruined not only my father's life, but also mine. I was seventeen when she left. I'd never recovered.

In his car, he started the engine, and asked, "What's wrong? Did I do or say something to upset you?"

I shook my head. "No, it's me." I looked him in the eye and wished I was someone else. "Look, I know you think you like me, but you just met me. You're leaving Sunday, right?"

"Yes."

"Then you should probably just go back to your life and count meeting me as a nice little memory."

"What if that's not what I want?"

"It's what *I* want. Besides, you don't live here. It's not like you're gonna come visit some girl you just met every weekend or something."

"How do you know that?"

"You have a job. You can't come back here when the season starts up."

He leaned across the center console and gently brushed my lips with his. "I can send for you."

"I-I have a life here. You expect me to drop everything for some guy I just met?"

He backed away from me and scoffed softly. "I'm not asking you to drop *anything* for me, Maria. I like you. You're pretty, you eat like a real woman, and you don't give a flip about me being in the NFL. Hell, you fascinate me. And I thought you liked me, too."

"I d-do."

"Then what's up with all the excuses? I just want to see you sometimes. That's it. I'll come see you, pay for you to come see me. Whatever bad thing you think is gonna happen, won't happen."

"Malachi—" My phone rang for the first time during our date, and I took the opportunity to check my screen and gather my thoughts. It was Felton, and it was after midnight. Felton never called me that late. "I need to take this," I said.

Malachi nodded.

I accepted the call, had barely said hello when Felton's panicked voice filled my ear. "Baby sis, you need to come to the hospital. It's Daddy."

six

"Faith to Believe"

I never liked hospitals. Not that I spent a lot of time in them or anything. My father had his ailments, but this was the first time they'd ever landed him in a hospital. My grandmother, his mother, had died at a ripe old age in her home, never having spent any time in a hospital to my knowledge. So had his father. The Browns, as a whole, were a group of healthy people with longevity embedded deep in their bloodlines. My mother's side—the Tripps—were another story. Cancer ran rampant on their side, but I was never close enough to any of them to visit them in a hospital or at their homes, for that matter. And we definitely didn't grow any closer after my mother left. So, sitting there in the ER waiting area would've been unpleasant and awkward for me even if it weren't my father who was being treated.

I leaned forward in my seat, glanced to my left at Malachi, who was a few seats away from me engaged in a hushed conversation with my brother, and then to the right where Spring sat with her eyes closed, her lips moving rapidly. I knew she was praying for Daddy. I wished I had the clarity and presence of mind to do the same. But my mind was clouded with what Felton had told me. I was trying my best to understand how it could be that my father was found outside, lying on his front lawn unconscious in the middle of the night. A friend had found him. Mr. Thomas was one of Daddy's oldest friends and often drove by the house at night to make sure all was well. Felton and I had thanked him but told him it was an inconvenience that wasn't necessary since Mr. Thomas lived on the opposite side of town. At that moment, I was glad he didn't listen to us.

My mind tumbled with thoughts and questions. What was Daddy doing outside? Where was he going? He never left his house, not even to check the mail, hadn't in years. Literally, years. I shook my head, wished I'd stayed home so I would've been closer to him. It seemed to take forever for Malachi to get us back into town. The ride had been quiet, tense. But I'd been glad for the excuse to be mute. Malachi was trying to move too fast, and it made me feel uneasy.

I should've just skipped out on the date and taken Daddy some ribs.

I shook my head and sighed. It was too late for should'ves. My daddy was in the ER for God knows what. And it was my fault. I never should have moved out.

"Hey, you need anything?"

I was so deep in thought, I hadn't noticed that Malachi had reclaimed his seat next to me. I looked over at him through exhausted eyes. "Only if you can make the doctor come tell me my daddy is okay."

"I'm sure he is," he said softly, earnestly.

I sat up straight and tilted my head to the side. "How can you be sure?"

"It's just a feeling I have. Everything's gonna be okay, Maria."

I leaned back in my chair. "Things haven't been okay for a long time. A long, long time."

He frowned. "Things don't look so bad from here. Your dad's got two great kids. His friends have been blowing your brother's cell phone up. He seems loved and appreciated to me."

I had opened my mouth to reply when a voice called my brother's name. I hopped up from my seat and rushed to Felton's side as the doctor approached him. Malachi followed me and rested his hand on my shoulder. The warmth of his touch seemed to ease my tension a bit.

"Well, we've got him stable now. Looks like it was alcohol poisoning."

I gasped. "What? Where'd he get enough liquor to poison himself? I mean, don't you have to drink a lot to get alcohol poisoning?"

The doctor, a tall, thin Middle Eastern man, nodded. "Well, binge-drinking is one cause of alcohol poisoning. But in your father's case, it's because of renal failure."

This time Felton said, "What?" He looked at me and must've seen the confused look on my face, because he promptly returned his attention to the doctor. "My father has renal failure?"

The doctor nodded. "I'm afraid so. We see this in a lot of diabetic patients. The fact that your father is a drinker didn't help."

I felt Malachi rest a hand on my other shoulder. He leaned in, and softly asked, "You okay? You need to sit down?"

I shook my head. "What does this mean? I mean, will he have to take dialysis?" I asked the doctor. I remembered a lady who used to frequent Brown Boy's a few years back. She'd come in to eat a couple of times a week after her dialysis. She used to tell me how she hated being on the machine for hours at a time, three days a week. She said she didn't really have a life. Daddy was basically a recluse. How was he going to handle having to go to treatment?

"Yes, we already dialyzed him here in the ER, and he's doing much better. A social worker will get in touch with whichever of you wants to be the point of contact and set up his outpatient treatment. They should be able to answer any other questions you have, too."

Felton asked if we could see him, and the doctor said it'd be a few more minutes before he could have a visitor.

As my weary mind tried to process the news, my legs weakened and the room began to spin. I would've fallen had a strong pair of hands not grabbed me—Malachi. As I collapsed in his arms and began to cry, he whispered. "I got you... I got you."

***

I fixed my eyes on the window as the sound of Daddy's soft snoring filled the small room. The sun had just risen, a new day had arrived, but the feelings of worry that had clouded my mind and my world for the better part of the last ten or so years of my life were ever present, taking the physical form of a dull headache. I rubbed my forehead and sighed. Felton and Spring had left after a short visit with Daddy. Malachi waited an hour before he left my side. I'd spent the night there, the only one left to take care of my father, as usual.

I couldn't shake my concern over the immediate future. I had spent what was left of the night and the early morning hours surfing the Internet on my phone, researching renal failure and dialysis. They had placed a venous access in his neck for his dialysis here in the hospital, but he'd eventually have to have a permanent access elsewhere, probably in his arm, and that would require surgery. Also, Daddy would likely be on a stricter diet now. This bothered me, because he never really followed his diabetic diet. There would be fluid restrictions. He'd have to leave the alcohol alone…for real. No more sneaking beers. He'd have to make all of his dialysis appointments. In short, he'd need close supervision if he was going to stay alive.

By the time Daddy's eyes fluttered open that morning, I'd decided to move back into the house with him. I had also decided to take some time off from Brown Boy's.

Daddy faced me and smiled. "You still here, 'Ria Rose?" he asked, referring to me by a name only he used, his special name for me.

My phone buzzed, and as I hit the button to send Malachi's call to voicemail, I said, "Yes, and I'm not leaving you, Daddy. I'm never leaving you again."

seven

"Take Care of You"

I was watching Daddy sleep later that morning when he appeared in the doorway. Tall, handsome, dressed in jogging pants and a t-shirt. I could smell a hint of his cologne from my seat across the room, and as exhausted and worried as I was, just seeing him eased some of the tension I'd been burdened with.

I managed a weak smile as I said, "Hi. What are you doing here?"

Malachi crossed the room and squatted beside my chair, peered up at me with intense concern in his eyes. "I came to check on you. Have you eaten? Been asleep?"

I shook my head. "No and no."

He glanced at Daddy and then stood, reaching for my hand. "Come on."

"Where we going?" I asked through a yawn.

"To get something to eat."

"I don't want to leave my dad."

"He's asleep, Maria. He won't miss you if you're gone for a few minutes. Besides, if you don't take care of *you*, you can't take care of *him*. Come on."

I didn't protest any further, because I honestly was starving. I don't know where I thought he was taking me. Well, I really didn't think about it at all. I just knew I was emotionally and mentally exhausted. So exhausted, that a few minutes after climbing into Malachi's rented vehicle, I was being shaken awake by him.

"We're here," he said.

I stretched my legs and rubbed my eyes, looked out the passenger window and smiled at the sight of Mother Millie's house. I was familiar with it as I'd attended many hospitality committee meetings there.

As Malachi led me into the house, the aroma of country sausage filled my nose. Mother Millie was seated at the kitchen table when we entered the room. Malachi pulled out a chair for me and then leaned over and kissed his grandmother's cheek. "Told you I'd be right back."

"You did, and you got Pastor's sister with you," she gushed, looking up from a newspaper to give me a warm smile. "I'm so glad you're here, Maria. How is your father, baby? I've been praying for him ever since the First Lady called and told me what was going on with him."

"He's okay. In good spirits."

"Mm, he's always been such a pleasant man, a good man. He helped me many a day when he was well. Pastor is so much like him."

I smiled rather than disagree with her. No one could hold a candle to the man my daddy used to be. No one. Not even my brother.

Malachi returned to the table and placed a plate overflowing with food in front of me. Mother Millie slowly rose and patted my shoulder as she left the kitchen. "Eat as much as you want. 'Chi, make sure she gets full."

"Yes, ma'am. I'll make it my personal mission." He sat directly across from me at the tiny, square table, setting a plate of food on the placemat before himself.

"You haven't eaten yet?" I asked.

"Yeah, but I'm not gonna let you eat alone. Besides, I could eat my granny's cooking all day long."

Mother Millie was known for her cooking. As a matter of fact, her dressing was nothing short of a culinary masterpiece. I could totally understand where he was coming from.

After Malachi said grace, we ate in comfortable silence. I was almost done when Mother Millie stuck her head in the kitchen door, and said, "I got the bed ready for you, baby. You can lie down whenever you're ready." She disappeared before I could respond, so Malachi was the recipient of my confused expression.

"I told her you spent the night at the hospital and that you need to get some rest."

"Why?"

His eyes widened. "Why? Because...I don't know. I guess I'm worried about you, Maria."

"*Why?*"

He leaned back in his chair. "What happened to you that made it so hard to accept kindness? Who hurt you?"

I'm surprised your grandmother hasn't already told you. But then again, Mother Millie wasn't one to gossip. "That's none of your business."

"Okay, I won't argue with that, but I hope you move past whatever happened. You're beautiful, and from your devotion to your father, I can see you're good. But whatever happened is pulling you down. You've got to stop letting that happen."

"Hmm, Dr. Phil the football player."

He shrugged. "I've got my issues, that's how I know you have yours."

I leaned forward. "Take me back to the hospital. *Now*."

He raised his hands. "Okay, look. I'm sorry. Let me just show you to the guest bedroom. If I let you out of here without taking a nap, Granny might actually whoop me."

I sighed and glanced toward the doorway. "I respect your grandmother and her hospitality, so I'm gonna stay, but you don't know me to be talking to me like this."

"Maybe I'm out of line…or maybe I just hit a nerve."

"Whatever. Just take me to the room." I rolled my eyes, stood, and followed him to a bedroom with a wrought iron bed covered in a gorgeous coral chenille spread. I climbed into the bed and was drifting off to sleep as Malachi covered me with a blanket.

***

When we left Mother Millie's house an hour later, she sent me off with a grocery bag full of her home-cooking. Tupperware containers were neatly packed inside and full of everything from chicken and dumplings to apple crisp. Malachi dropped me off at my house, where I put the entire sack in the refrigerator, showered, dressed, and took my car back to the hospital. Spring and Felton were in Daddy's room when I arrived, and they were all laughing and joking until I appeared. I couldn't help but wonder what about my presence seemed to turn everyone in my family's joy into sorrow when I seemed to have the opposite effect on Malachi. There was rarely an occasion when he didn't wear a smile on his face. Maybe my folks thought I was too serious. But someone had to be. Felton took things too lightly, always had. When our mother left and our father fell apart, Felton was living and working out of state. I was only seventeen and felt so alone back then, but no matter how many times I called and begged Felton to come home, he wouldn't. He thought I was being overly dramatic about Daddy's condition. It took him two years to finally come visit, and upon seeing our Father and his growing alcohol problem, he had to admit I was right.

If me being around shifted the mood, then so be it. Someone had to take care of Daddy, and that someone would obviously have to be me. And it would've been ill-advised for anyone to get in my way.

eight
"Here for You"

Malachi dropped by the hospital to say goodbye the next morning. Something had come up, and he had to leave earlier than planned. He apologized like we were in a committed relationship and had made important plans or something.

"You don't have to apologize for going back to your life. It was good to meet you," I said, as we stood by a window in my father's hospital room. Daddy was asleep, and since he was asleep the day before when Malachi came to visit, they had not met each other. Not that they necessarily needed to. What were Malachi and I to each other anyway? Almost, but not quite, friends? We were more of a thought than anything.

He placed his hands on my shoulders, sending a surge of unfamiliar warmth through my body. I wanted to jerk away from his touch but not nearly as badly as I wanted to feel more of it.

"I'll be checking on you and your dad. I…" He dropped his eyes from mine.

"What?" I asked softly.

"I don't want us to lose touch. There's something about you that keeps you on my mind."

"Sorry," I said sarcastically.

"It's not a bad thing. Not a bad thing at all." He leaned in and let his lips gently brush my right cheek. "Call me, okay? Any time—day or night. I got training camp coming up, but I'll call you back if I can't answer when you call."

"Okay...I will." It wasn't until he'd left and several hours had passed that I realized I didn't have his phone number. I hadn't given him mine, either.

***

"You sure you're okay? Brother Wilkins said you can use his wheelchair. I don't know why you didn't let me go over there and get it," I said, as I watched my father negotiate the front steps of his house on shaky legs.

"I'm fine, Maria! I'm fine. But you making me nervous with all this hovering! Move back some, or you gonna be the reason I fall."

I sighed heavily. My normally sweet father had been irritable since the second he left the hospital and climbed into my car, telling me he could've driven himself home and he wished I'd brought his truck and how he hated the CD I was playing and why didn't I stop by Brown Boy's and get him some ribs and on and on...

My head was throbbing by the time he'd shuffled through the house to his easy chair in the living room.

"You need groceries," I said. "I'll go get some."

He threw up his hand at me. "Okay. Bring a two-liter Coke back with you."

"Daddy, you know you can't have that."

"I'm a grown man! If I want some Coke, I'ma have me some Coke!"

Tears sprung to my eyes. My father had never, *ever* yelled at me before. "Daddy…"

He didn't turn and look at me or say another word. So I just left and cried all the way to the grocery store. I still didn't buy him the Coke, though.

When I got back, a couple of his friends, Mr. Ball and Mr. Simmons, were in the living room with him carrying on a loud and lively conversation. When I stuck my head in the door to tell Daddy I was back, he informed me that he was going over to Mr. Ball's house for dinner. I had dinner alone in my old bedroom.

I endured two days of my father's nasty attitude before I decided to return to work. I called my uncle and told him that for now, I'd just work the days Daddy didn't have dialysis. As mean as he was being to me, I was still going to make sure he didn't miss his treatments. Felton arranged for Daddy's helper to come when I was at work.

"Hey, stranger!" Tanay, one of the waitresses, greeted me with the second I stepped into the restaurant. "How's your daddy?" She pulled me into a hug so abruptly that I almost got a mouthful of her braids. Her strong perfume transferred to my clothes, and I knew I was going to spend the rest of the day smelling like her.

I stepped out of her embrace, and said, "He's better. At home now and ornery as all get out."

"Well, maybe he just needs time to adjust to everything. Mr. Felix said he's got to do dialysis now?"

"Yeah. It's been hard on him knowing he's got to do it from now on. They said he's not a good candidate for a kidney transplant with his other…issues, so they won't put him on the list. The only way he can get a new kidney is if a family member is a match and volunteers to give him one, and he refuses to even let me or Felton get tested."

"Hmm, well, I'll keep him in my prayers. What about you? How are you handling things?"

I leaned against the counter and glanced around the empty restaurant. In another thirty minutes, we'd be opening for business for the day. "I'm making it."

"And how is the football player?"

"Wow, really?"

She tilted her head to the side and pursed her pink-painted lips. "I saw how he looked at you in here last week. So…"

"He's fine."

"So I heard…and saw."

I shook my head. "I mean, he's nice. We had a good time while he was here. Now he's gone back home, and that was that."

"That was that? Y'all are over?"

"We never started, Tanay."

"Oh, yes you did. He had lunch with you like three days here, took you out, and sat with you at the hospital…"

"How do you know about the date and the hospital?"

"The same way I know he also took you to his grandmother's

house. This is a small town, and people love to talk."

"I see. Folks need to get a life, and we need to get to work."

"While you back in that kitchen working, I want you to think about this: that man likes you, *really* likes you. A man like him with that much money wasn't up in here three days in a row for the atmosphere. The food is good, but it's not *that* good. And don't you tell Mr. Felix I said that."

I chuckled.

"He likes you, Maria. And you know it. I don't know why you're playing dumb, but you need to stop."

I rolled my eyes as I left and happily took my post in the kitchen. I wasn't at all in the mood to be around people.

***

A note on the refrigerator informed me that Daddy was having dinner with Felton and Spring, so I decided to go check on my own house. As soon as I walked in, I remembered the food Mother Millie had given me and swiftly unpacked the sack and began microwaving the chicken and dumplings. I was about to fold the paper sack up when I noticed a piece of paper lying at the bottom. On it was a note that read:

Here's my number. Use it anytime.
-Malachi

I smiled and grabbed my cell phone from the counter. Without a second thought, I dialed the number. I was surprised when he answered it on the first ring. "Hello?"

"Hey, it's Maria."

"Hey! So, you found my number. Took you long enough."

"Yeah. Just getting to that food. Um…how are you?"

"I'm good, great now that I hear your voice."

I blushed and adjusted the phone on my ear.

"I miss you."

My smile grew wider. "I miss you, too," I admitted.

"Well, you should."

"Wow…"

With a smile in his voice, he asked, "How's your dad?"

"Feeling good enough to give me hell every day."

He chuckled. "That's a good thing, right?"

"I guess, and he's suddenly got a social life. Been having dinner away from home nearly every night."

"Well, maybe being so sick made him want to live a little more. Your brother told me he was kind of reclusive before."

"He was. You and my brother talked a lot when you were here, huh?"

"Me and him have more in common than you think."

"I guess. Well, I just wanted to give you a call. I'm-I'm about to eat my dinner and get back over to my dad's house."

"Okay, beautiful. I'm locking your number in."

Another smile graced my face as I watched the timer on the microwave count down. "Good."

nine

"Heart to Yours"

"What are you doing?" he asked.

I sat on the side of my bed and glanced at myself in the dresser mirror. "Nothing…getting ready for bed. What are you doing?"

"Talking to you."

"Wow, I haven't heard that since grade school. Really corny, Mr. Douglass. I thought you were smoother than that."

"Are you questioning my smoothness, Miss Brown? I was smooth enough to get your attention…and your number."

Through a grin, I said, "And you think that makes you smooth?"

"I know it does, because I know you don't give your number out to just anyone."

"Hmm, you know that, huh?"

"Yes…and let's not mention the fact that you went on a date with me. From what I hear, I broke some kind of record or something with that one."

"Mm-hmm, you might wanna stop getting your information from my brother. Contrary to what you might think, he doesn't know *everything* about me."

"He knows enough. His information put me way ahead of the

competition."

"Competition?"

"Yeah, from what I hear, there are some members of your church who've got it bad for you."

"Good Lord. Felton needs to stop. Do the two of you talk about anything other than me?"

"Yeah, we talk about the Bible, football, goals, a lot of stuff."

"What goals do you talk about? Winning the Super Bowl or something?"

"That's one of my goals, but it's definitely not at the top of my list or worth having a conversation about."

"Then what is?"

"Having you in my life."

My cheeks began to heat up. "You don't have to say stuff like that if you don't mean it."

"Oh, I mean it, Maria. There's nothing more important to me right now than getting to know you and growing closer to you."

"Um…that's pretty intense considering we only just met."

"I'm the type of man who doesn't mess around when he sees what he wants. You're exactly the type of woman I want to be with—beautiful, smart, loving, and real. I like you, Maria, and if you give me half a chance, I'll love you."

I closed my eyes and lay back on my bed. "Malachi…I don't know what to say."

"Say you'll give me half a chance."

"I will…I am. More than half," I said softly. "I—uh—like you, too."

"I wish I could look into your pretty eyes right now, see that smile of yours you're so stingy with. I know you think I'm crazy for saying this all the time, but I really do miss you."

"I miss you, too."

"Then come see me."

"I-I can't. Not until I'm sure my father is okay. He has his dialysis and—"

"I understand. Look, I have training camp in a couple of months, so I'll be busy with that. After training camp, the season starts. My schedule will be crazy then. I'd like for you to come sometime in the next couple of weeks. You can stay here with me, or I'll get you a room. Doesn't matter. Whatever makes you the most comfortable. I wanna show you Dallas and introduce you to my family and friends. I wanna wine and dine you, make you feel like the queen you are. I wanna treat you so good, you won't wanna go back to Arkansas. But I won't pressure you. Take your time, but don't take too much time…"

"Malachi—"

"You don't have to say anything right now. Look, it's getting late and I know you said you have work in the morning, so I'll let you go. Talk to you tomorrow?"

"Yes…goodnight."

"Goodnight."

I ended the call and padded down the hall to check on Daddy, who was fast asleep. He was being marginally compliant with his diet and fluid restrictions, hadn't refused any dialysis treatments, and was snapping at me much less frequently. Things were going pretty well at home and at work for me, but I did miss Malachi. He'd made such an impression on me during his brief time in Beckton that his absence had left an almost tangible void behind. I enjoyed talking to him on the phone nearly every day, but it wasn't the same. He'd been gone for three weeks, but it felt like three years. I wanted to see him, to take him up on his offer so badly, but I refused to abandon Daddy and leave him at the mercy of Felton and Spring. They didn't understand Daddy, not really.

Feeling deeply conflicted, I closed my eyes and prayed aloud, "Lord, help me. Strengthen me from the temptation to abandon my duties to my father. Help me to do the right thing for him and for me. I love you, Lord. In Jesus' name, amen."

ten

"When Sunday Comes"

It was my Sunday to drive the church van, a task I usually didn't mind, but I woke up on edge that morning. Well, actually, I woke up feeling fine until Daddy copped an attitude with me over breakfast. I just didn't get it. The more I tried to help him and accommodate him, the more I tried to appease him, the worse he behaved. It was almost as if he didn't want me there, and it hurt to think that was even a possibility. For so many years, it was me and Daddy, as close as a father and daughter could be. I was his rock, and he was mine after Mama left. We were all each other had, but now it seemed our once iron-clad bond was broken.

Everything irritated me after breakfast. I couldn't find anything to wear that I liked, and then I arrived at the church to find the van's gas tank on *E,* which meant I had to fill it up before driving all over town to pick up the people who had requested rides. And then Sister Delaney was running late. That wasn't a surprise, as she was always running late, hence she was always last to be picked up. But her tardiness got on my last nerve this time, because I knew by the time we made it to church, worship would be half over.

I was totally frustrated when I finally entered the sanctuary to find it packed. There was not an empty seat in sight, so I had to sit in the balcony, and I hated climbing those stairs, but nevertheless I did. I closed my eyes and tried to calm myself as the words from the tail-end of a song the choir sang soaked into my brain. They sang about praising God in advance of a blessing. They sang about taking Him at His word. They sang of keeping the faith, all things I was struggling with. Honestly, I had been struggling with having faith my entire adult life, but who could blame me when I had to witness my father's steady decline all those years?

By the time Felton stepped up to the podium, I was feeling better. Not one hundred percent myself, but much calmer. "Good morning, brothers and sisters. It's a blessing to see so many souls in God's house today!" Felton declared.

Amens echoed throughout the sanctuary.

"I'm just thankful He saw fit to let me see another day! How about you?"

Another round of amens.

"I won't be before you long, but I have a word to share with you all this morning. Turn with me if you will to the Gospel of John, chapter ten and verse ten, and let us read it out loud together: 'The thief comes only to steal and kill and destroy; I have come that they may have life, and have it to the full.' Amen! I want to speak with you this morning about living a truly full and abundant life."

I focused on my brother's words with a new sense of alertness. I let his words settle not only in my mind but in my heart. He talked about how being less than God intended us to be and not using our talents was an insult to Him. How playing small and shrinking into the background not only robs us, but also the people we were put on earth to bless. He said living abundantly meant to take advantage of every opportunity God places before us to let our light shine.

He ended with, "Your life is a ministry. What kind of sermon are you sharing? One of bold faith or one of fear?"

His words were on my mind as I drove the members back to their homes. What kind of sermon was I sharing? I was taking care of my father, just like I always had, but was there more I was supposed to be doing, and if so…what? I had no education, no skills, and I hadn't used my talent for art in years. What would an abundant life look like for me?

***

Dropping the van riders off after church always proved to be a much more difficult task than picking them up. Since most of these folks had no other form of transportation, they made requests for me to stop by a store or drop them off somewhere other than their homes. Some locations were familiar to me, others weren't, but I did my best to oblige everyone. I was well-beyond exhausted when I returned the van to the church and parked it in its covered parking spot. It was late afternoon by the time I climbed in my car and headed to Brown Boy's to pick up dinner for me and Daddy.

Despite my weariness, I ended up sticking around the restaurant and helping them for more than an hour, because they were totally swamped with the after-church crowd. The dining room was full, and they had so many call-in orders it was ridiculous. By the time I made it home, the whole day was gone, and I was sure Daddy had already eaten some leftovers and was in bed. As I sat in my car for a moment, trying to gather the energy to step out of it and into the house, a text message came through from Malachi: *Hey, I missed talking to u today. How was church?*

Me: *Good. Had van duty today and then I went to work for a little while. I'm so tired.*

Malachi: *Man, I wish I was there to take care of u. Still missing u.*

I smiled as I replied with: *Missing u, too.*

Malachi: *Get some rest. Talk to u tomorrow.*

Me: *OK. Nite.*

Malachi: *Nite.*

Grinning so hard my cheeks ached, I quietly entered the house and put Daddy's food in the refrigerator, intending to eat mine in my room and then collapse into bed. The living room was dark as expected, but as I made my way to my room, I heard what I first thought was the TV playing in Daddy's room, voices. It didn't take long for me to realize one of the voices was actually Daddy's. The other was female. Did Daddy have a woman in his room?

I shuddered at the thought. I hadn't known my daddy to have a girlfriend or female friend at all since my mother left us. Then I remembered how neat and clean the kitchen was when I put Daddy's food in the fridge, and it occurred to me that it was probably his aide. I mean, I had literally been gone all day. I was grateful she'd stuck around so late to be with Daddy.

With my food in hand, I headed to Daddy's room to thank her. The smile I wore when I entered the room quickly dissolved when I saw my mother sitting next to my father's bed.

eleven

"Stranger"

I couldn't move.

All I could do was stand there and stare at her, my heart close to beating itself to death. It'd been so long, ten years, since I'd been in the same room with her, and at that moment, all I could think about was the mess she left behind and how in one act, she had diminished my father to a shell of a man and completely broken my heart and ruined my idea of love.

She stared at me with a look I couldn't readily describe on her face—shock? Awe? Fear? I heard Daddy say something I couldn't focus on or make out, because it was as if I had tunnel vision on my mother and everything else around me was a blur, including Daddy's voice. She stood from the chair. Her mouth was moving, but I had no idea what she was saying. She inched toward me. I almost instinctively moved backward while shaking my head.

"You're not here," I whispered.

Sound returned to my ears in time for me to hear her say, "Yes, I am, 'Ria Rose. I'm here." A single tear rolled down her weathered face. She hadn't aged well from what I could see.

"Don't call me that."

"'Ria Rose, now calm down," Daddy said, having shifted from lying in bed to sitting up.

"What is she doing here?" I asked, my eyes still on my mother.

"I had Felton call her. I don't know how much longer I'ma be here, and I wanted to see her."

My eyes finally left her face and met my father's eyes. "Don't say that."

"It's true. The only thing keeping me here is those dialysis machines. Maybe I'll be here another twenty years, maybe not, but I know it's time for me to get things in order. It's past time for me to get things square with your mother. So that's what I spent most of today doing."

"Square? What are you talking about?"

"I forgave her."

"What?"

"And I don't want you to wait until you're half dead to do the same thing."

I shook my head. "I'll never forgive her! She ruined my life! She needs to go!"

"She ain't going nowhere. We got us a good understanding. She's staying…for good."

"What?!" I screamed.

She moved toward me again with a look of anguish on her face, extended her hand and rested it on my cheek. Some stupid part of me wanted to lean into it and relish in her touch. But the rational part of me snatched away from her.

"Please, Maria. I've missed you so much," she said in a quivering voice. Tears wet her face. "Oh, you haven't changed a bit. You look so young, like my little girl."

Tears wet my face, too. I didn't know what to do other than turn and run from the room, through the house, and out to my car.

***

I spent the next twenty-four hours holed up in a hotel room ignoring repeated phone calls from my father and Felton and Spring. I had forgone my own home for the hotel, because both Felton and Spring had a key and I was pretty sure they'd already busted into my house. I couldn't deal with them, any of them. I knew Felton had orchestrated this little reunion. He had always sympathized with our mother, spent years trying to get me to see her side. I told him I saw her side clearly. She saw something she wanted and deserted her entire life to have it. Her side had cast a huge shadow over my life. Her side manifested in my father becoming a pitiful hermit of a lush and me being left to clean up behind her. Whatever Felton thought he knew or understood, he was wrong. He wasn't around when our family imploded. How much vomit did he have to clean up? How many soiled sheets did he have to wash? How many times did he have to help Daddy into the shower? How many nights did hearing Daddy wail in despair bring tears to his eyes?

None.

Not one.

I sat on the bed in my hotel room and glanced at my buzzing cell phone. This time, it was Uncle Felix, who was probably wondering why I wasn't at work. I couldn't deal with work or people or even being in this hick town another second knowing it was only a matter of time before my family located me. So without a suitcase or a penny to my name, I drove to the airport in Little Rock and parked in long-term parking. I was still sitting in my car when I dialed his number.

"Hey! I was just thinking about you!" He sounded so bright and jubilant it brought tears to my eyes.

"Hey," I said in a tremulous voice. "Does your offer still stand? You still want me to come see you?"

"Yes, I really do."

"Well, I'm at the airport, but I...I don't have any money on me. I spent my last on a hotel room and I left my credit cards at home but I can't go home right now and all I have is my ID and my cell on me, and I don't even have the charger for that, and—"

"I'll book you a ticket for the first flight out. Give me a few minutes, and I'll call you back with the information."

"Okay, thank you."

twelve

"Higher"

One of the first faces I saw after stepping off the plane in Dallas was Malachi's, still impossibly handsome, tall, and fine in a black t-shirt, black jeans, and an expensive-looking pair of white sneakers. I was so relieved to see a familiar face that wasn't related to me, I was tempted to run to him, but opted to walk swiftly into his open arms. He pulled me to him, rubbed my back as he said, "Hey, hey…you okay?"

I rested my head on his chest and closed my eyes. "No, but I'm much better now." I looked up at him, felt a fluttering in my stomach, and had to admit he did something to me no one else had ever done. Made me feel sensations that were foreign to me, took my mind to some rather uncomfortably physical places.

"Thank you so, so much," I said, as I fought to control the desire to kiss him and cry at the same time. "I just need time and space. I can't be around my family."

He nodded as he released me, glanced around, and then took my hand. "For a second there, I forgot you don't have luggage, was gonna ask you about baggage claim."

"Yeah, I just wasn't thinking. I-if you have a washer and dryer—what am I saying? Of course you do. Well, I'll just wash my stuff every day."

He stopped in his tracks and looked me in the eye, which made me drop my gaze to the floor. "How many days you plan on staying?" he asked.

"Uh-um-I-uh, I don't know. A-a few days?"

"Then we'll get you some clothes."

"No, you don't have—"

"It's not a problem, Maria. As a matter of fact, we can do that now. Or are you hungry?" He checked a watch that looked like it was made of nothing but diamonds. "It's getting close to lunch time."

My stomach rumbled as we stepped into the parking deck, so I said, "Yeah, I think we should eat first. I skipped breakfast."

"All right. We can drop by the house. There's plenty of food there."

I nodded and almost gasped when he stopped at the passenger door of a silver Rolls Royce and opened it for me. "This is yours?" I asked, and then felt dumb for asking.

"Yep. Hop in."

It was hard for me to hide my awe or contain my excitement as we took the smooth-as-butter ride through the city. My eyes stretched wide as I took in the buildings and cars, so many cars. So much traffic. Such a contrast to Beckton.

My daddy had never been one to travel. He didn't see the value in it. I often speculated that my daddy's unwillingness to travel, his staunch reclusiveness, was the reason my mother not only left our house, but the entire state, fleeing to Chicago with a new lover to start a new life. People would say, "That Rhonda Lee always was wild, couldn't stand to be in one place for long."

For a second, the thought crossed my mind that maybe she wasn't wild, maybe she just wanted to feel what I was feeling at that moment. Maybe she wanted to see and experience something bigger than the four corners of Beckton, Arkansas.

Up until this little impromptu trip, the biggest place I'd ever seen was Little Rock, Arkansas. Little Rock was a village compared to Dallas. Dallas was faster, shinier, and much, much bigger. When I caught my mouth hanging open, I quickly closed it and glanced at Malachi.

"It's something, isn't it? First time I saw this city, I fell in love with it. I'm so thankful my mama made the move here when I was a kid. We struggled, had to stay in the projects, but it opened my eyes to so many possibilities."

"Yeah," I said, as I gazed out the windshield at the road full of cars ahead of us. I felt like a child on the first day of school, or someone who'd been locked in a room for most of their life, finally released into the world and feeling the sunshine on their face for the very first time.

I eyed the interior of the car, took note of the clarity of the music pouring through the speakers. I'd never ridden in a car that expensive before. I don't even think I'd ever been in a new car as opposed to a used one. "This is a really nice car," I said, as I stuck my hand under my thigh, touching the creamy leather of the seat.

"Thanks. Just got it a few days ago. You're the first person to ride in it with me."

I smiled.

We made it to his house, his *mansion*, a while later. "I have never ridden that long and been in one town the whole time," I said.

He pulled into his garage next to three other cars and hopped out to open the passenger door for me. "Yeah, traffic is especially bad right now. Sorry about that."

"It's okay."

We entered his house through a door that connected the garage to the kitchen. For a bachelor's house, it was spotless, but then again, I was sure he had a housekeeper. Probably had a gardener and a cook, too. One look at the food he pulled from the refrigerator as I sat at the kitchen table told me I was probably correct about the cook. Still, I asked, "Did you cook all that?"

He pulled a container from the microwave. "No, but I can cook. Just prefer not to."

"I love to cook. Maybe I'll fix you something while I'm here."

"I'd love that. Hey, I meant to ask if you want to stay here or if you want me to get you a room at a hotel. There's plenty of room here and I'd love for you to be here with me, but I want you to be comfortable"

"I can stay here. And thank you again. I'm sure Felton told you what happened."

He set a plate before me, said, "He told me your parents reconciled."

I cringed. "I guess that's one way of putting it."

He sat across from me with his own plate. "And you're obviously not happy about it."

I dropped my eyes to my plate. "Is this roast beef? These potatoes look good."

He reached across the table and grabbed my hand. "You don't have to talk about it now if you don't want to. But you have to eventually. It's not good to hold stuff inside."

"I know."

He was still grasping my hand when he said, "Let's bless this food and eat."

***

After lunch, Malachi gave me a tour of his 10,000 square-foot, five-bedroom, six-bath home. It was gorgeous, a virtual palace full of expensive furniture. Every room was spotless and smelled heavenly, as if each one had been bathed in a different scent. "You live here alone?" I asked.

He nodded as he led me back down the stairs. "Yep."

"You planning on having a big family or something?"

"That depends on how many kids you're willing to give me."

I blushed, stopped, and leaned against the banister. "Is that a proposal?"

He was standing at the foot of the stairs when he said, "If it was, would you accept it?"

"I plan to be in love when I get married."

"So do I."

"Are you saying you're in love with me?"

"I'm saying I plan to be."

I descended the last two steps and stood in front of him, tried not to feel all warm inside at the way he gazed down at me. "You can't plan love, Malachi. It just happens."

"Well, I respectfully disagree, Maria. I planned to be the best player on my high school and college teams, to play for the Cowboys, and to get my family out of the projects. I also wanted you to come to Dallas. I made all of that happen because when I make a plan, I don't stop until it comes to fruition. We're going to fall in love, Maria Brown, and you're going to be my wife and eventually, the mother of my five or six kids."

I scoffed. "You act like I don't have a choice in any of this. I mean, you're nice and you've been kind to me, but you can't *make* me fall in love with you."

He stepped closer to me, leaned in, and kissed my lips. Then he said, "When the time comes, I won't have to make you do a thing."

thirteen

"The Way You See Me"

I really felt some kind of way about Malachi buying me clothes. I also felt some kind of way about me letting him. But the thought of being in Beckton, where I had plenty of clothes, made me feel worse. So, I accepted his generosity with a promise to pay him back as soon as I returned home, whenever that was. I really wasn't sure when I'd be ready to go back or if I'd ever be ready to deal with my family, my mother.

My mother.

As I sat in Malachi's enormous guest bedroom with Lane Bryant sacks nearly covering the huge bed, the image of her standing before me filled my mind. She looked as much the same as she did different. Same medium brown skin, long, thick hair that she straightened and kept pulled back into a ponytail at the base of her neck. Crows' feet now accented her dark eyes, and her once full face was thin, almost gaunt. So was she. In a loose-fitting jogging set, she looked so much smaller than she had all those years ago. I wondered if she still had the hour-glass figure, the same one she'd given me. I'd just spent years piling pounds onto mine, giving me an almost pear shape that made it hard for me to find flattering clothes.

I eyed the sacks full of size-sixteen t-shirts and jeans and wished I'd bought something cuter, sexier. There was a red, off-the-shoulder A-line dress I saw that I liked. I had tried it on in the dressing room while Malachi sat on the little sofa in the store and played with his phone. Sexier-than-should-be-possible Malachi, who had snatched the attention of every woman in the place. The workers had fawned over me because I was with him. He'd seen the dress when I picked it out and told me he liked it. I put it back, because it reminded me of something my mother would've worn back in the day to some party she would've had to drag my father to. I put it back, because I didn't want to be her. But I *was* her. I'd run away and left Daddy, too.

No, Daddy had betrayed me. He had turned his back on me and everything we went through together, the years of shared misery and pain. He'd wiped away our bond by forgiving her for the unforgivable. I was right. I was the only one who was right.

I should've gotten the dress.

A knock at my door startled me, so it took a few seconds for me to say, "Come in."

It was Malachi; of course it was Malachi. "Let's go out for dinner," he said, with a grin on his face.

"Uh...okay. Sure. Now?"

"Yeah, but the place is dressy. So you'll need to change."

My face fell. Why didn't I get the dress?

He was still grinning. I almost wanted to cry. "Well, I didn't get anything dressy, Malachi. I'm sorry. I just didn't think..."

He frowned slightly. "What about that red dress?"

He had no idea what I'd bought. He just sat on the sofa and handed me his credit card, signed the slip when I handed it to him. That had really impressed the ladies behind the counter. They must've thought I had it going on, especially when he grabbed all the bags with one hand and my hand with the other when we left. They had no idea what a pathetic charity case I was.

"I-I didn't get it."

He sighed. "Hold on a sec." He left and returned with three more Lane Bryant bags in his hands and an even wider grin on his face. He placed the bags at my feet.

"What is this?" I asked through bleary eyes. I was really about to cry about the clothes I bought or didn't buy. Or maybe I just needed to cry for some arbitrary reason.

"After we got back here, I called and bought all the other stuff you tried on over the phone and had the lady at the store bring it here."

I glanced down at the sacks, saw something red in one of them, and instinctively knew it was the dress. "Why?"

"Because you didn't get enough stuff. You don't know how to accept a blessing, Maria. Thought I'd help you out."

I shook my head. "Thank you," was all I could say.

"You're welcome. Get dressed. I'm hungry."

***

Malachi had to take me to a shoe store on the way to dinner since neither of us had thought to get me any dressy shoes. I found a pair of black heels pretty quickly. Malachi bought the same shoe for me in every color they had in stock in my size. I wasn't sure how I felt about that.

Dinner was actually a dinner party at the house of one of his teammates. As he pulled into the circular drive and waited behind a line of cars for the valet, my eyes took in the scenery—the massive Tudor-style house, the limos and cars, the tall, impossibly thin women on the arms of the huge men.

"Why'd you bring me here? I won't fit in," I said softly. I could feel him looking at me but didn't turn to face him.

"Says who?" he asked.

"Look at these people. Look at me, and tell me I fit in with them."

"You fit in with *me*. Look, I'm not leaving your side, Maria. It's my boy, Al's, wife's birthday. Al was one of the first guys to befriend me when I was picked for the team, and his wife is an angel. They're church-going and down to earth. I wanted to be here for them...and I wanted you with me. I want you on my arm. Nobody else."

I sighed and turned to face him. "Why?"

"You know why. Because you're gorgeous and I like you, and to be honest, you need this. You need something other than barbecue joints and church."

"How do you know what I need?"

"Look, you're here for a reason, a real reason."

"Because I had no place else to go."

"That's not true. You have a home. You might have been running from your family, but you came to *me* for a reason."

I sighed again. "Okay, why do you think I came to you?"

"Because you like me, too. And a part of you wants to know what a life with me will look like. Well, baby, I'ma give you the grand tour while you're here. Starting right now." He stretched across the console of his Rolls and gently kissed my cheek.

I wasn't sure if it was the kiss or hearing him call me baby, but I couldn't think of another word to say other than, "Okay."

As we stepped out of his car, him in a navy-blue suit and me in my red dress, I had to admit we looked good together, and it felt good to feel his hand on the small of my back as he guided me to the front doors of the house.

The inside of the house was gorgeous in a way different from Malachi's home. The décor screamed the fact that a woman lived there. His place was nice, but Al and Davina Hegemon's house felt more lived in, but that was probably because they had three kids and one on the way. Al was a humongous man, at least six-foot-five, and hulking with wide shoulders, dark skin, and he was strikingly handsome, almost as handsome as Malachi. Davina was a tiny five-feet-even with golden brown skin and what I assumed was honey blonde weave that flowed down her back. Even with a protruding belly, she wore a tight little black dress and heels but was still dwarfed by her husband in his black suit. They looked so mismatched, but I guess the same could be said of me and Malachi by some. Him, a tall portrait of fitness, and me, much shorter and a little more than chunky.

The couple welcomed us with open arms and appeared truly excited to meet me.

"Well, damn," Al said when Malachi introduced me to him. "I think this is the prettiest woman I've ever seen you with. Man, how you get her to agree to come with you?"

I smiled graciously. It wasn't that I'd never heard that I was pretty before, but it was usually coupled with *just like your mother*, so I ended up blocking the sentiment out for most of my life. It was nice hearing it come from someone who didn't know her. And it was nice not having him add the other tag people liked to attach to it—*for a big girl*.

Malachi clutched my hand and perused the room, introducing me to so many people, I lost count. They all seemed nice enough, and things were going well until Davina swooped in and separated us. "Malachi, you need to stop being selfish and let me introduce Maria to the other ladies."

He looked at me, probably saw the panic in my eyes, and said, "Wait," while trying to pull me from the grip she had on my hand.

"You can have her right back," she said, as she pulled me away, then leaned in close to me and whispered, "I'm so glad you're a sister. These other Negroes act like they're allergic to black women. You'll see."

And I did. A minute or so later, she introduced me to a small group of women—most of whom were Hispanic, white, Middle Eastern, anything but black. And they were all literally the same trophy wife-type—thin, huge boobs, heavily made up, plastic. They were nothing like me with my wild, thick, natural hair or my chunky body, and I hated how young I looked, like I still belonged in high school. And why didn't I at least try to put on some make-up other than lip gloss?

They greeted me with awkward smiles as they hesitantly extended their diamond-drenched hands to shake mine. Even the two or three black women in the bunch were eyeing me warily.

"So...you're with Malachi?" a tall brunette asked.

I nodded. "Yes."

I didn't bother to elaborate that we were just friends, because among these women, I wanted us to be more than friends since I knew they thought he was out of my league. I could see it in their eyes. I wouldn't give them the satisfaction of being right.

"Oh..." the Middle Eastern-looking one said.

I was so uncomfortable, my skin felt loose, like it no longer belonged to me.

"Well...I guess he's moved on from Candice then," said a light-skinned black woman with long raven hair, wearing a black dress so low-cut you could almost see her nipples.

I wanted to know who Candice was, but I knew this woman was trying to get under my skin. She had succeeded, but I wouldn't let her know that. "I guess so," was my response.

Her eyebrows flew up, and in my periphery, I could see Davina smirking.

At that exact moment, I felt a set of arms snake around my waist and a head rest on my right shoulder. "There you are," Malachi said into my ear, planting a kiss on the side of my neck.

I grinned at his perfect timing, turned my head, and looked at him out of the corner of my eye. "Hey."

"You miss me?" he asked, as he buried his face in my neck. I was sure this was an act for the benefit of the ladies, but my body didn't get the message. I was feeling sensations I'd never felt before. So when he turned me around and kissed me, I wrapped my arms around his neck and kissed him back.

"Come on," he whispered, after our lips parted. "Nice seeing you, ladies," he tossed over his shoulder as we walked away.

Once out of earshot, he said, "Let's get out of here. They're only serving finger food, and I'm so hungry I'm about to die."

I giggled. "I'm hungry, too, so you won't get any arguments from me."

***

We ended up at McDonald's, where he signed autographs for the crew through the drive-thru window. Later that night, as I lay in his guest bed, I thought about him and me and how it felt to be on his arm and in his arms. How it felt for his lips to be on mine. It was all so foreign to me. It had been years, high school, since I had a boyfriend because my life had been consumed with my father and trying to take care of him, and look where that got me. I liked Malachi, and not just because he was nice and sent for me when I asked. I liked him as a man. A man whose arms I longed to be in at that moment, because I just needed that, had never really had it, and although I hadn't known him long and this was my first night in his home, I also needed *him*. So I slipped out of bed and down the hall, knocking lightly on his door, hoping he was staring into the darkness just as I had been moments earlier.

"Yeah…come in."

I eased the door open to see him sitting on the side of the bed watching TV. He was shirtless with a sheet covering the lower half of his body, and the sight of well-defined muscle in his gorgeous shade of brown made my breathing halt for a second. I wondered if he was naked from the waist down, too.

He grabbed a remote from beside him on the bed and turned the TV off. "You need something?" he asked.

Everything in me wanted to say, "You." But instead, I said, "Can I sleep in here…with you?"

He grinned. "You scared to sleep by yourself?"

I shook my head. "No, I-I missed you."

His expression grew serious as he patted the empty portion of the bed. "I missed you, too. Hop in."

I felt so awkward climbing into his bed wearing one of the many Cowboys t-shirts he'd given me. He turned the lamp on his side of the bed off, plunging the room into darkness as I climbed in and pulled the covers over my body.

He didn't touch me, but settled into his side, and said, "Goodnight," for the second time that evening.

"Will you hold me?" was my reply.

"I'd love to."

With my back to him, he spooned himself behind me, kissing the back of my scarf-covered head.

"Malachi?" I whispered.

"Yeah?"

"I'd—I want—I want to be with you. Like as your girlfriend." I sounded like a first grader. I felt like one, too.

He tightened his grip on me, and I could hear the smile in his voice. "You know I want that, too. But are you sure?"

"Yes, I am."

"Okay…anything else you want?"

"Yes, I want us to go grocery shopping tomorrow so I can cook for us. No more McDonald's."

He chuckled lightly. "All right. Hey, you know what this means, don't you?"

"What?"

"If you're my woman, you can't go back to Arkansas, at least no time soon."

"I wasn't planning on going back."

Fourteen

"It's Alright, it's OK"

Lying in Malachi's bed early the next morning, I smiled. I'd never spent the night with a man before, and it felt absolutely wonderful to be in his arms. I missed him, even though I knew he'd just gone to the store and would be back in no time, or so he said.

I stretched across the bed and grabbed the remote from the table next to his side, turned the TV on, and began surfing the many channels. Then I stood and looked out the window at the backyard, trying to grasp the fact that I was his girlfriend.

Me.

I grinned at the memory of the ladies' faces at the party when he hugged and kissed me. Then I put a finger to my lips, trying to recall how his had felt against them.

"Hey, I got you a toothbrush and the toothpaste you wanted."

I spun around to find Malachi standing just inside the room holding up a paper sack.

I walked over to him, took the sack, and said, "Thank you," kissing his cheek and almost skipping into the bathroom.

He followed me as I opened the toothbrush and ran hot water over it. "Your brother called me…again."

I squeezed toothpaste onto the toothbrush and put it in my mouth so I wouldn't have to respond.

"You should call him."

I shook my head *no*.

"I know you don't want to, but I need you to do it for me."

I finished brushing my teeth, rinsed my mouth out, grabbed a towel, and wiped my face. Finally, I said, "What do you mean?"

"He said if he doesn't hear from you today, he's calling the police and telling them I kidnapped you."

I looked at him and saw that he was dead serious. "What?!"

"Look, I know nothing will come of it because it's not true, but I don't need that kind of publicity."

I slipped past him out of the bathroom and walked back over to the window. Shaking my head, I said, "I'll call him. I cannot believe this! What kind of preacher is he to threaten to lie like that?"

He stepped beside me and grabbed my hand. "He's worried. I suppose he'll do anything to make sure you're okay."

I sighed. "Yeah."

I called Felton right after breakfast. Sitting on the sofa in Malachi's living room while Malachi went to the grocery store with a list I'd made, I felt all kinds of anxiety when the phone began to ring in my ear. My stomach flipped when Felton answered. "Hello? 'Ria?"

He hadn't called me 'Ria since we were kids. He must've really been worried. I didn't care. "Yeah, it's me. What do you want that's got you threatening Malachi?"

"I'm gonna apologize to him for that."

"You should. Right now."

"I know...I was desperate. Daddy is worried sick about you."

"I'm fine. Malachi has been very kind to me."

"I don't doubt that, but it was really selfish of you to take off like that without letting us know where you were going."

"Well, you figured it out."

"Maria, you need to stop acting like this. Daddy's upset. Mama's upset..."

I hopped to my feet and began pacing the floor. "What?! You can't possibly think I care about her feelings! She never cared about mine! And Daddy will be okay. He got his wife back just like he always wanted."

"Maria, you've got to let this stuff go. Get over it! It's been years, and you're still holding a grudge against your own mother! You need to grow up!"

I scoffed. "Oh, I've *been* grown! I had to grow up real quick when *your* mother disappeared! But I wouldn't expect you to understand. It was out of sight, out of mind for you. You weren't there to experience it. None of it really affected you."

"They're my parents, too! You think their divorce didn't affect me? You think I wasn't upset? You think it hasn't bothered me to see how Daddy dealt with things?"

"Maybe it affected you in some way, but you weren't there to pick up the pieces like I was! You didn't come home for years after she left. How much vomit did you have to clean up? How many bounced checks did you have to cover? How many sets of soiled sheets did you have to wash? Did you have to listen to Daddy cry himself to sleep at night? Watch him drink himself half to death? I was a teenager and I had to deal with all of that stuff by myself and still go to school, and going to school was hard enough because I had to face all of my classmates knowing that they knew my father was a lush and my mother was a whore!"

"You need to watch your mouth talking about my mama!"

"She's my mama, too. And she *is* a whore! What else do you call a woman who sleeps with her daughter's boyfriend?!"

"Maria—"

"No! You wanted to talk? Let's talk! Let's talk about how she slept with my eighteen-year-old boyfriend for months. Months! And then announced a week before my birthday that she was leaving with him! She left my father for my boyfriend! Married him and started a life with him! And what did I get? I got to watch my father fall apart. I couldn't even deal with my own heartbreak. It hurt. It cut like a knife for her to do that to me. So don't talk to me about respecting her. She never respected me!"

"Look…will you just call Daddy? Let him hear your voice?"

"No!"

Before he could say another word, I ended the call and collapsed onto the sofa, looked up to see Malachi standing a few feet away from me. At the sight of him, I burst into tears.

***

He held me tightly in his arms as tears poured from my eyes. I wasn't sure if the tears were coming because of my conversation with Felton or because I was sure Malachi had heard me. I was embarrassed, ashamed of my family history, and I was sure he was regretting ever getting involved with me.

"I'm-I'm sorry," I mumbled, as I pulled away from him.

He gave me a warm smile. "No need to be sorry. Will you tell me what's going on with your mother now?"

"Didn't you hear?"

He nodded. "Yeah, but I can tell there's more. Tell me, Maria. You've been holding this inside for too long. You don't deserve to carry this alone. Share some of your burden with me."

Fresh tears filled my eyes at the tenderness in his voice. "I'm so ashamed…"

"Don't be, baby. Just tell me. I'll never judge you."

I took a deep breath and leaned into him. He wrapped his arms around me and lay back on the sofa with me nestled safely in his embrace. "Tell me," he repeated.

"Um…okay. I've-uh-only had two boyfriends in my life—you and a boy named Terrance Watson. I was-I was crazy about him. He was a year older than me, and we started going together when I was fifteen. Back then, my life was normal. Felton was off at college. My daddy still worked and preached revivals and as a guest at some churches on Sundays. Mama did hair part-time. They would have parties from time to time, and eventually, I started working at Brown Boy's and Terrance got a part time job at a grocery store, but we always made time for each other.

"A year into our relationship, Terrance started pressuring me for sex. I was raised to wait and believed virginity was precious."

"It is," Malachi softly said.

"Yeah, well, he wasn't trying to hear that. He was relentless. I mean, after a while it was all he talked about, and we couldn't kiss without him trying something. Finally, two years into our relationship, he threatened to break up with me. I thought I loved him, so I gave in, and I felt horrible about it afterwards. It just felt wrong.

"A few days later, I woke up in the middle of the night to my parents arguing. That wasn't new. They did that from time to time, because they were just so different. They were truly mismatched, but I thought it was like magnets with them. You know, opposites attract? They'd fought through more than twenty years of marriage together. But something about this argument was different. It sounded much more intense to me.

"I got up and left my bedroom, heard the voices growing louder, coming from the living room. I headed down there, but to this day I don't know why. Daddy was screaming at her, asking her how she could do whatever she'd done. When I made it to the living room, I saw my mother sitting on the sofa crying. There was a suitcase on the floor next to her. I'll never forget the tears rolling down her face. I'd never seen her cry before; she was always this carefree person. Always dancing around the house or laughing and talking on the phone.

"Neither of them realized I was in the room. She was whimpering, saying she didn't mean to fall in love with him, but she did. I had no idea who *him* was at that moment. Not until there was a knock at the door and I heard him call for her to come on. Of course I knew his voice, so I walked right past my parents and opened the door.

"Terrance's eyes bugged when he saw me standing there. It was around two in the morning, so I guess he figured I'd be asleep. He mumbled something about being there to pick up Rhonda. He called my mother by her first name, and that made my blood run cold.

"I started screaming at him, asking him what he wanted with my mother. He told me they were in love, had been for a while. I guess I forgot my parents were there or I didn't care, because I asked him if he was in love with her when we had sex. He said yeah, that he just did that to see if he really loved my mom. Decided he did. My mom left with him that night, and my world fell apart. My father started drinking, stopped preaching. I have spent my life since she left taking care of him. I can't do it anymore, not if he wants her in his life after the way she ruined both his and mine."

"Baby…I'm so sorry. I'm so sorry," he softly said. "Dear Lord, heal her pain. Please, heal her pain…"

I couldn't say another word. I just lay there in his arms and let my seemingly endless tears flow.

I felt lighter after I shared that portion of my past with Malachi. Over the next few days, I did a lot of talking about my feelings—anger, sadness, and from time to time, hopelessness. In talking to him, I realized I'd never really dealt with my own pain. Daddy's pain had taken precedence, and honestly, everyone saw me as a teenager, a little girl in puppy love who lost her boyfriend. They decided I'd get over it and just left me to deal with it alone. Felton, Daddy, everyone just dismissed me and what I went through, made it seem insignificant. Daddy was the only victim in this, not me. But no matter how they saw it, it was a big thing to me to lose my mother and the boy I loved all at the same time. Honestly, it was devastating.

It felt good to get it out and cry it out and have Malachi there to listen and wipe my tears and hold me, but it also made me feel like a burden.

"I'm sorry," I said after the third time I broke down. Or maybe it was the fourth time. There were so many tears shed those few days, things tended to blur together. "You've got to be tired of this."

He shook his head, cupped my face in his hands, and said, "You lost people who were important to you, Maria, and you never got to mourn them. You deserve the chance to mourn, and tears are a normal part of that process. And after the weeping comes the joy, so says the Word. So I'm going to sit right here and help you through the mourning, and then I'm going to rejoice in your healing with you."

Well, that only made me cry harder. Through my sobs, I whimpered, "Why are you being so nice to me?"

He pulled me tightly into his arms. "Because it's time for someone to take care of you. I'm that someone. I care about you, Maria. I really do."

"But why?"

"Because it's what you need."

"Thank you."

"You're welcome, baby."

fifteen
"Blessings"

He held my hand in the car the entire ride to church the next Sunday. I had to fight not to stare at him in his suit. I'd always had a thing for men in suits, but seeing a man with a body like Malachi's dressed in his finest was a whole different experience that I didn't think I'd ever get used to. My goodness, this man was gorgeous! Even more gorgeous than he'd been in that suit at my church in Arkansas. Gorgeous and *mine*. It took a while for that to sink in. It'd been more than two weeks since I'd made the declaration to him that I wanted to be his girlfriend. I guess I had to see past my own misery to really get it, but he was my boyfriend, my beau, my *man*. At that moment, it occurred to me that I'd never had a man before. My only other boyfriend was literally a boy. But Malachi? There was nothing juvenile at all about him.

He squeezed my hand in his. "We're here."

I looked up to see us pulling into the parking lot of a huge church, one that was familiar to me because I had watched their broadcasts on TV with my father. Although he stopped preaching or attending church after my mother left, he never missed Pastor James Cloud's TV sermons. Before each broadcast, a picture of this very church would appear on the screen while the show's theme music played. "You belong to Abundant Faith Tabernacle? Reverend Cloud is your pastor?" I asked.

"Yeah. I've been a member here for a few years now."

As he parked, I stared out the window at the mass of cars crowding the lot. "My father is going to have a fit when I tell—" I cut myself off when I remembered I wasn't talking to him.

"You should call him," Malachi said, as if he'd been eagerly awaiting the opportunity to make the suggestion.

I looked at him and shook my head. "I can't. Not right now."

He raised an eyebrow. "But you will, right?"

"Sooner or later…"

"I hope you do. Listen, you know I leave for camp soon, and I can't take you with me."

"I know…but I can stay at your house, right?"

"Yeah, of course you can, baby."

I felt a fluttering in my stomach every time he called me that, wondered if it would ever get old, hoped it wouldn't.

"But, you'll be alone. You need to reconnect with your folks so you'll have someone to talk to."

I frowned slightly. "You can't call me while you're gone?"

"Yeah, but it won't be the same. We've been spending all this time together, sleeping together. I'm gonna miss you. I think you'll miss me, too."

"I will…"

"You know Davina, and you'll meet my mom today, but you need your family."

I sighed and rested my gaze on my hands, which were folded in my lap.

He reached over and lifted my chin so that I faced him. "Just think about it. Okay?"

I nodded. "Okay."

***

Besides the cameras that were clearly evident and the sheer size of the place, being inside Abundant Faith felt like being inside any other church, and growing up a preacher's kid who became a preacher's sister, I'd been inside plenty of churches in my lifetime. The people were friendly, and I blushed every time Malachi introduced me as his lady, didn't miss the wide-eyed looks that some of the people gave him when he made that revelation. I wasn't what they were expecting. Shoot, I wasn't what *I* expected him to want, either. And he wasn't what I expected at all—handsome with probably the best heart I'd ever known a person to possess besides my dad. But my dad's heart had been broken so badly…

As I took a seat next to Malachi near the front of the sanctuary, I decided to clear my mind of the mess I left behind and focus on my future, because I knew there was a future for me with Malachi and I wanted it. I never wanted to stop being his lady. I missed my friends and family, but I didn't want to go back to the drudgery and depressing life I'd lived for so many years, even though I'd once believed it was the best life for me. I didn't even realize how miserable I was until I distanced myself from my life as it was. Now I knew better. It wasn't just the mansion and the Rolls or the money he freely spent on me. It was being with him, lying in his arms, listening to him pray for me. It was Malachi.

It was love.

That's what I felt when I was with him. Oh, I'd always known love from my family. But what Malachi generously gave me was different. It made me smile and feel tingly all over, and I liked it so much, I didn't want to stop feeling it. I never wanted to leave him.

As I shifted my focus to the huge, ridiculously good choir, I smiled. Malachi grasped my hand in his and my smile widened. Yes, this was what I'd been missing. Malachi was right. I needed to be here with him. I needed to feel what I felt when I was with him. I really did.

After Rev. Cloud gave a stirring sermon about what it truly means to love our neighbors, Malachi took me all the way to the podium to meet him. Although I'd watched the tall, magnetic man on TV for years, I was so nervous when we approached him, I was actually shaking.

"Pastor, good morning," Malachi greeted.

"Malachi!" he said, in a booming voice that didn't really require a microphone. The handsome man with deep chocolate skin and an alarming white smile embraced Malachi before turning his attention to me. "And this is Maria? The young lady you told me about?"

Furrowing my brow, I glanced at Malachi who wore a sheepish expression.

Pastor Cloud laughed. "It wasn't anything bad. As a matter of fact, he came and saw me when he first got back from Arkansas to tell me he believed he'd found his future wife. Glad to finally meet you."

Now I was even more nervous. "Oh…uh-um, it's an honor to meet you. My father never misses your TV sermons."

He winked at Malachi. "She comes from good stock. Good choice, Malachi."

Malachi grinned. "I know."

"Your father's back in Arkansas?" he asked me.

"Yeah…yes, sir. He's not well right now."

He gave me a serious look as he grasped both of my hands. "I'm going to pray for his total healing and restoration, and I expect to get a praise report straight from his mouth. You be sure to bring him here to meet me when he's better, because he *will* get better, in Jesus' name."

I smiled. "I will. Thank you, Pastor. Thank you so much."

If I wouldn't have been running the risk of my mother possibly answering the phone, I would've called Daddy and told him about meeting Pastor Cloud, shared with him that the charismatic preacher's smile was just as bright in person and that his words had even more of an impact as I sat under his anointing, and I definitely would've told him he'd been added to the esteemed orator's prayer list, but I couldn't take that chance. I didn't want to hear her voice as she sounded pitiful and asked for forgiveness I didn't want to extend to her. I wanted life to be like it was before, when she was out of sight and mostly out of mind except for the stinging reminders of why she was absent. I was used to them, and they had even dulled in the years since she'd left, but seeing her and hearing her voice felt like pouring salt in a healing, but still open, wound. All the feelings of betrayal and anger—no, scratch that. It was hate that I felt for her. Right or wrong, I absolutely despised my mother, and hearing her voice would only intensify that hatred.

"So, you enjoyed service?" Malachi asked, pulling me out of my thoughts.

I glanced at him sitting behind the wheel of his car, racing down the highway or expressway or whatever it was we were on. "Yeah," I said, "I loved it! Thanks so much for taking me."

"Yeah, I try not to miss a Sunday, but I've been slacking lately. I know we missed last Sunday, but we won't miss anymore."

"We?" I said, trying not to smile. I failed.

He glimpsed at me with a grin on his face. "Yeah, me and you...*we*. We're a thing, Maria, in case you didn't know."

"I know…" I dropped my eyes and closed them as a now familiar warmth spread over my body.

"And we're gonna keep being a thing, baby."

"For how long?" I asked.

"Forever."

I loved the sound of that.

I'd almost forgotten we were having lunch with Malachi's mother when he parked the car in front of a beautiful, ranch-style house. It was not as spectacular as Malachi's house, and it was much smaller, but it was still nicer than any house I'd ever stepped foot in back home.

"We're here," Malachi said, as he turned the car off.

I scanned the driveway, noting three other cars. Something told me they weren't all his mother's. "Who all is here?"

"Everyone."

My eyebrows flew up. "Everyone like *who*?"

"My mom, my two sisters, and my two brothers, plus their families."

"Your whole family?"

He nodded. "Yeah."

I sighed lightly. "Okay…"

He reached over and grasped my hand. "You nervous?"

"Yes. I thought I was just meeting your mom, and I was already nervous about that. I don't know about this. I…"

He squeezed my hand. "You're my girl, right?"

I smiled and wondered to myself why it felt so good to hear him say things like that. "Yes."

"Then you should meet my family. I met yours."

"I know, but—"

"And like I said, I want you to have some support when I leave for training camp since you intend to stay in town. Or maybe you could go back to Arkansas to see your folks…"

I shook my head. "Nope."

As I reached to open the passenger door, he stretched his arm across me and grabbed the handle. "You're my girl. You don't open doors when you're with me. *Ever*," he said, and then leaned in and kissed me softly on the lips.

When we parted, I murmured, "Uh…okay."

We walked hand in hand through the unlocked front door of his mother's house and were greeted by smiling faces crowding the foyer of the home that smelled like I'd stepped back in time and into my own family home. The faces before me were warm and all shared a familial similarity to Malachi's, but as attractive as his siblings all were, Malachi still stood out as the most beautiful among them.

"Everyone, this is my girl, Maria Brown. Baby, these are my sisters, Janice and Cheryl, and my brothers, Jacob and Dwon. That's Dwon's wife, Kelisha, and his little girl, Dwona. That's Jacob's wife Tierra and their twin boys, Michael and Jordan. That's Janice's husband, Steve. And Tierra is holding Cheryl's baby girl, Namibia."

I smiled as I was pulled into hug after hug, all the while wondering to myself if I'd ever get everyone's name straight.

"Where's Mama?" Malachi asked, as he grabbed my hand again.

"In the kitchen waiting for her baby boy," one of his brothers replied. I think it was Jacob.

Malachi kissed my cheek. "Come on, baby."

"It was nice to meet y'all," I said, as he pulled me away.

Their collective words of agreement sounded jumbled as he led me to the kitchen where a tall, thin woman stood at a huge, stone-topped table removing shiny cardboard covers from rectangular foil pans.

"Ma?" Malachi said softly.

The woman looked up and a smile identical to Malachi's spread across her face. She was a pretty woman who probably looked older than she really was. There was an edge to her looks, like she'd lived a hard life and seen a lot of things she wished she could erase from her memory. She stepped into her big, tall son's arms, a look of adoration on her face. "My baby!" she gushed.

I smiled and felt like maybe I was intruding on an intimate moment between the two of them, but Malachi reached for my hand before his mother even released him.

"Ma," he said, as he pulled me close to him. "This is Maria. Maria, this is my mom, Tina Douglass."

Before I could utter a word, she pulled me into a hug and squeezed me with more strength than her small frame revealed her to have. Then she backed away and held my face in her warm hands.

"Oh, my! You remind me of Ms. Two when she was younger. She had a body that could stop traffic, too."

I blushed and dropped my gaze a bit. "Uh…thank you."

"Oh, she's shy, too? How sweet! Well, all I can say is you got you a good man in my son. He's one of the best."

I lifted my eyes. "Yes, ma'am. He is."

She smiled at me. "She does sound like back home, Malachi!"

He grinned at her and then fixed his eyes on me. "I told you."

Dinner with the Douglass's was really nice. The food came from a local soul food restaurant, as his mother revealed to me that she stopped cooking years ago. The atmosphere was light, but boisterous, and a blind man could see how much everyone at the table loved Malachi. Even the children kept leaving their little table and attempting to climb into their famous uncle's lap, only to be scolded by their parents. I truly enjoyed the great food and warm reception.

Once in his car, on the way to his place, he said, "So what do you think about my people?"

"I think you have a terrific family who loves you to death."

"Hmm, that's the same thing I thought when I met your family."

I fell silent. I really wished he'd stop bringing them up.

"Baby, I didn't mean to upset you, but it's the truth."

I glanced over at him. "I know what you're trying to do, but don't. Today was a good day. Don't ruin it for me, for us."

He sighed. "All right, Maria. All right."

After a few moments of silence, I asked, "You told your mom I sound like back home?"

"Yeah, you do. You feel like back home, too."

"What does that mean?"

"Hmm, we were poor when we lived in Arkansas, but no other place has ever felt the same to me. When I think of home, I think of comfort, warmth, and love. That's what I feel when I'm with you, Maria."

I smiled as I gazed out the passenger window of his car.

One thing I didn't ever think I'd get used to was Malachi's kisses. They were so gentle but urgent, almost like he was just as much a novice at it as I was. But I knew that wasn't the truth. A quick Internet search had told me he'd had many girlfriends, including that Candace girl the women kept mentioning at Davina's and Al's house.

We were in his bed that night, holding each other close, our mouths linked, my heart beating fiercely in my chest. Malachi made me feel so…so alive, as if I'd been flailing through life barely breathing all those years before him. I guess, in a way, I had been holding my breath, waiting for something, something that would jolt me out of the monotonous gloom I had been existing in. And maybe, just maybe, that something was Malachi Levi Douglass.

Maybe…

His lips vacated mine, and he murmured, "I'm not sure how much longer I can do this with you, Maria."

I searched his face in the darkness of his bedroom, and with a deeply furrowed brow, asked, "Do what?"

"Kiss you and touch you without making love to you."

"I'm-I'm sorry. I don't—"

"No, you don't have a reason to apologize unless you want to apologize for being beautiful and sexy."

"Sexy?" I laughed.

"What's funny?" he asked softly. "I'm dead serious about that."

I shrugged as I placed my hand on his muscular chest and felt the steadiness of his heartbeat. "I don't know. Just never had anyone call me sexy before."

"I don't know why not. You're just my body type, curvy, soft, *gorgeous*."

I kissed his cheek. "Thank you."

After a beat or two of silence, I said, "We can do it. I mean, I want to do it with you." I sounded embarrassingly like I was a kid. That offer had to have turned him completely off.

"You've only done it once, right? In high school with that guy you told me about, the one your mom married?"

"Yeah…" There in his arms, I hated being reminded of her, of *that*.

"Then really, you're still a virgin, baby. We'll wait and make it special when we do it."

"Okay. Do you want me to stop sleeping with you? Will that make it easier for you?"

"Not really. I'll just lie in here missing you."

"I'd miss you, too."

"Then I'll deal with it until the time is right."

If I'd had the nerve, I would've admitted how badly I wanted him, confessed that I probably wanted him more than he wanted me. But I wasn't brave or bold enough to speak my mind about something like that. So instead, I snuggled into his body and my stupid mind told me to say, "Tell me about Candace."

"What? Why?"

"I don't know…those women, the other wives, kept mentioning her at Al's and Davina's."

"I dated her and it didn't work out."

"How long did you date her?"

"I don't know…five or six months."

"Why'd you break up?"

"We weren't compatible. We were looking for different things in life. Like, I was looking for someone I could settle down with. She was looking for a baller, someone with money."

"Oh…did you love her?"

"No."

"Did she love you?"

"Definitely not."

"And she was a gold digger?"

"Yep, basically."

"Did you spend a lot of money on her before you broke up?"

"Um, a little. Too much if you ask me, since she never offered me anything in return."

I hesitated, and then said, "But you buy me things, and I haven't done anything in return."

"I *want* to buy you things, Maria. I like taking care of you."

"Like you take care of your family?"

"No, it's different with you."

"How?"

"I always felt kind of obligated to take care of them, to get us out of the 'hood, you know? But with you, I just…I look at you and I can feel your pain, baby. I knew from the moment I first saw you when you introduced me at your church that you'd been carrying a burden for a long time. I felt it in my spirit that there was this shadow cast over you. There was this heaviness that was holding you down and keeping you from living the life God wants you to live. I looked into your eyes and thought to myself that something was suffocating you. I just want to help you breathe again, Maria. For you and for me."

Tears crowded my eyes. I'd never heard anything so beautiful in my entire life. I'd never felt anything in my heart and soul as pure as what he'd just said to me. "Malachi…"

"Maria, the people who were supposed to make you feel safe and cared for turned the tables on you and made you a caregiver long before you were equipped to do it, and baby, that was so unfair to you. But now I'm here, and I'm convinced that God sent me back to Arkansas, to that church, on that day…for you. I know it's not a coincidence that it was you who introduced me or that your brother took me to eat at your uncle's restaurant while you were working there. This was all in His plan. Us being together is in His plan. Me loving you is in His plan, because I love you, Maria. I love you, and all I wanna do is love your pain away."

I sniffled. "I don't understand why, though. What could I possibly offer you in return? I'm a nobody, Malachi. I have nothing. I have no education. I have a regular job. I'm not sophisticated. I don't even know how to put on make-up right. This is the first time I've been outside the state of Arkansas in my entire life. I'm broken, still holding on to hurt and anger from years ago. I'm messed up. Why in the world would you want me?"

"I want you because of everything you just said. Like I told you before, you're real. You're not an illusion. Your body is real; your heart is real. If you ever love me, I know it'll be pure. You don't want anything from me, actually feel guilty about the things I do for you. And you were wrong when you said you haven't done anything in return. You keep me grounded, and in the midst of the craziness of my life, you remind me of what really matters in this world—love and home and genuine people. Things can get surreal for me with the fame and the women throwing themselves at me. You can lose touch with reality, you know? You remind me that there are still real people out there besides my family. I love you for that and for just being you."

"I love you, too."

He squeezed me tightly in his arms. "See, I told you you would."

sixteen

"Beauty for Ashes"

I'd been in Dallas long enough to start repeating outfits, and for some reason, that really bothered Malachi. So much so, that he took me shopping again. This time, he took me to Ashley Stewart upon my request. I had shopped their online site but had never been in one of their stores, so I was excited to see what they had to offer. And I didn't even feel guilty about letting him buy me more clothes. I thought of it this way: I was his woman, and I was more than certain he wanted me to look my best if for no other reason than to look good on his arm. Okay, so I knew that wasn't exactly it. I knew he had a good heart and just liked doing things for me, but that little scenario made it easier for me to accept his kindness.

We entered the store and hadn't been in there a full minute before some woman approached him, screaming at the top of her lungs. She whipped out her phone and shoved it at me, requesting rather loudly that I take a picture of him and her together. She was all over him, and while he looked more than a little uncomfortable, I was downright angry about her touching my doggone man. So I just stood there with a frown and stared at her, and a few seconds later, she snatched her phone from me and took a quick selfie with him. She attracted so much attention that poor Malachi was bombarded with fans. People poured into the store from outside, as I was sure the folks inside had shared that he was in there. When he was finally able to break free of the crowd, we ended up having to leave empty-handed.

He wore a look of frustration when we climbed into his Mercedes Benz SUV and sighed as he started the engine.

I reached over and placed my hand on his cheek. "I'm sorry. I can just order some stuff online."

He shook his head. "I should've known better. I mean, we've been lucky this hasn't happened before." He sat there behind the steering wheel for a moment, and then said, "I'm still gonna get you some more stuff, and I think I have an idea how we can do it without all of this craziness."

I leaned over and kissed him. "Okay."

A few hours later, past their closing time, we stepped back into Ashley Stewart. Malachi had called and arranged for us to shop after hours. They had accommodated us, even setting a chair outside my fitting room so that I could step out and model for him like I had seen women do in the movies. It was fun seeing his reactions, how he'd whistle or widen his eyes when I stepped in front of him wearing something he liked. A couple of times he stood and spun me around before kissing me, or pretended to lead me in a dance right there in the store. The short, plump, blond clerk grinned as she observed us, and when it was time to check out, she said, "I don't think I've ever seen anything as cute as the two of you before in my life. It must be nice to be that much in love."

As he handed her his credit card, Malachi wrapped an arm around my shoulder and kissed my neck before saying, "It is. It really is."

***

Standing before the huge mirror in Malachi's bathroom, I appraised myself in my new black, belted kimono dress that stopped just above my knees and black, open-toe sandal heels. I had spent the better part of the morning twisting my natural hair with Malachi watching as intently as he probably did game footage, and the resulting twist-out was gorgeous, if I do say so myself.

Waiting for me in the living room, Malachi wore a pair of dark gray slacks and a white shirt. When I entered the room, he stood and grinned at me. "Yeah, that's one of my favorite dresses."

As I walked into his arms and kissed him, I replied with, "Thanks for buying it for me."

"I should've bought you ten of them so you can just wear them around the house. Shoot, I just might do that."

I giggled. "You're crazy."

"I know."

This time when he told me he was taking me out to eat, he meant to an actual restaurant, no sneak-attack friend or family gathering, thank goodness. He took me to a place called Miśarana, a trendy restaurant that served fusion cuisine.

Once we were seated, I kind of just sat there and stared at the menu, having not even a hint of a clue what I should order.

Probably sensing my confusion, Malachi said, "They have a wide variety of really good dishes here. Choosing something just depends on what you like. Do you like Indian food? If so, their Indian fusion dishes are great."

I lifted my eyes to meet his and felt my cheeks heat up. "Malachi…I've never had Indian food before. I've had Chinese and soul food and fast food, but not Indian or fusion or anything like that." I was sure I sounded just as bewildered as I felt. Bewildered and out of place. A true fish out of water. Thoughts of inadequacy invaded my mind. What was I doing there with him? I didn't belong there…I belonged back in Arkansas in an apron at Brown Boy's. I knew greasy barbecue. I knew country living. This life was foreign to me.

He reached across the table for my hand, making me jump a little. "Baby, are you okay?"

I shook my head and blinked back tears. "No."

With a deeply furrowed brow, he softly said, "You wanna leave and go somewhere else?"

"No, you can stay. I don't wanna ruin your night. I can…I can get a taxi back to the house or something."

He fell against the back of his chair. "Maria, what are you talking about? You think I'd send you home in some taxi and sit here and eat without you? Baby, you're the only reason I wanted to go out in the first place. So you've never had Indian food before. So what? That's the whole point, baby, for you to experience something new. Years ago, I'd never had it before, either. Everyone has a first time for everything. I wanna experience all your firsts with you. Will you let me?"

I gave him a tiny smile and nodded. "I'm sorry. I just...I feel out of place, Malachi."

He looked me in the eye, and said, "Look at me. You are not out of place. Your place is with me, right where you are. You hear me? Keep your eyes on me, and don't worry about anything or anyone else. Okay? I love you."

"I love you, too."

"Good, now that we got that out of the way. You like shrimp? If so, try the coconut shrimp. It's the bomb."

I grinned. "Okay."

seventeen

"Livin'"

I set a plate of ham, eggs, home fries, grits, and toast before Malachi, kissed him on the cheek, and then took a seat across from him at the table and bowed my head as he said grace.

"Father, thank you for this food prepared by my lady's gorgeous hands. May it nourish our bodies and give us strength. In Jesus' name, amen."

I smiled at him as he dug into his food, shoveling a spoonful of cheesy grits into his mouth and declaring, "Mmm, girl, you're gonna make me marry you *today* cooking like this!"

I shook my head as I dug into my own food.

I had planned to fry some chicken that evening, but Malachi wanted to go out again, determined to expose me to as many culinary experiences as possible before he left me for training camp. The next day was Davina's baby shower, and we had made plans to go shopping for a gift, but I had a better idea, something that had been on my mind for several days.

I took a sip of orange juice and looked at him, smiled when I saw he had basically inhaled his food. Not much was left on his plate. "Malachi, you think we could go buy a sewing machine and some fabric today? I think I want to make a gift for Davina instead of buying one."

"Sure, baby. Whatever you want."

"Okay, and you don't have to go in the store with me. I mean, if you don't want to."

"Why wouldn't I want to?"

"The fans and stuff…"

He gave me a wide grin. "You worried about me? I'm a big boy. I'll be okay. I ain't leaving your side until I have to."

We were on our way to Stitches and Hems, a fabric store I'd found on the Internet, when the call came through. Even though the radio was pretty loudly playing a Kendrick Lamar song, Malachi still noticed the incessant buzzing of my cell phone, and asked, "You gonna get that?"

"No."

"Why? Do I need to get ignorant up in here? Is that some other dude calling you?"

I nodded. "Yep, my brother."

"Oh."

I was surprised Malachi let it drop, but I suppose he was tired of beating the "you should talk to your family" dead horse.

When the voice message alert popped up on the screen, I hesitantly placed the phone to my ear and listened:

"Hey, sis. Uh, I guess you're doing okay. You looked good in those pictures Anika showed me when I went to Brown Boy's yesterday. You look really happy. I guess Malachi's taking good care of you. Spring said to tell you she missed you. So do I, and Ma and Dad. We all miss you, sis. Wish you'd call sometimes. Anyway, I just called to check on you and to tell you that Ma and Daddy are getting remarried this Saturday. I'm officiating the wedding. They really want you to be there. Call me for details. Love you."

Married? I didn't even know my mother and Terrance were divorced.

I slowly pulled the phone from my ear and peered out the window, realizing we were parked in front of the store and that Malachi was staring at me. *When did we get here?*

"You okay?" he asked, as he released his seatbelt.

I shrugged. "I don't even know how I feel right now. It seems my folks are getting remarried."

"Yeah, I know. Felton called and told me earlier this morning while you were still asleep. Asked me how I thought you'd take it. I told him the only way to know that was for him to call you."

I sighed.

"You wanna go to the wedding?"

"No!"

He held up his hands. "Okay…okay."

I glanced at him. "I'm sorry. It's just…you don't get it. No one does."

"No, I get it. Your mom hurt you. But, baby, you're gonna have to forgive her, for you. I had to do the same thing with my father. I hated that man for years. Me and my brothers and sisters all have the same dad, a married man who never left his wife, barely gave my mom a dime over the years, was never any kind of father to any of us. I hated being poor and hungry and wished him dead so many times, I'm actually embarrassed about it now. There was so much hatred inside of me, it almost killed me. And then one day, God spoke to me, told me if I didn't forgive him, I was never going to be any better than him, and all these dreams I had weren't going to mean anything if I didn't let this go. So, I did. I forgave him. I even called and told him I forgave him…" He paused and shook his head. "He didn't pretend that he cared and asked me what I was forgiving him for. It did nothing for him, but it freed me. You need to do this so you can be free, too."

"I-I will eventually. Thank you for sharing that with me."

"You're welcome, baby. You ready to go inside?"

"Yeah." I reached for the car door handle and then dropped my hand.

"You almost opened that door, huh? You know better."

I smiled as I watched him walk around the front of his car and open the door for me.

***

I set up my sewing machine in the guest room that had been my bedroom for about ten seconds and smiled at the sacks full of fabric and thread sitting on the floor beside me. I'd also bought some patterns. My mom had taught me how to make my own patterns years ago, but I didn't trust my skills with that just yet.

I spent most of that day making a cute little pink dress with matching panties and had started on a mint green set when Malachi dragged me out of the room to get ready for dinner. I had skipped lunch altogether, having found it easy to slip back into the joy of a hobby I had deserted years ago. I was stepping out of the shower when my phone lost its mind with successive beeps coming through, indicating several back to back text messages. I wrapped one of Malachi's bath sheets around my body, sat on the padded bench at the foot of the bed, and checked my phone.

Tanay had sent me several pictures—pictures of me and Malachi leaving Ashley Stewart after our first attempt at shopping there, one of me kissing him in his SUV outside the store taken from somewhere in front of the vehicle, as the view of us was through the windshield, a picture of us having dinner at Miśarana. My mouth fell open. So these were the pictures Felton was talking about? What in the world?

I quickly tapped out a message to her: *Where did u get these pictures?*

Tanay: *They were posted on the Top Ballers page on Instagram. They're calling u Malachi Douglass's mystery lady. From the comments under the pictures, folks are excited to see him with a real woman. Ur a star, girl!*

Me: *Girl, please. I'm just me. Same old Maria.*

Tanay: *Honey, u are more than just u. U are Malachi Douglass's girl! I'm so proud of u! And I'm jealous. Real jealous.*

I shook my head.

Me: *Ur so crazy. Hey, I gotta go. Getting ready to go out to eat. I'll get back with u later.*

Tanay: *Oooo, I can't stand u! I can't remember the last time I went out to eat!*

Me: *Hmm, sounds like u need to get u a Malachi ;-)*

Tanay: *I know that's right!!!!*

I tilted my head to the side as I observed Malachi studying the menu. We were at a French restaurant called La Rose Soyeuse, and when he offered to order for me, I offered no resistance. I truly trusted his judgment as much as I did everything else about him, especially his heart. His heart was by far his best feature. I smiled as I thought about how comfortable I felt around him now, as if I'd known and loved him my whole life. Everything about us, about me and him, felt so...so right and pure and beautiful. Everything about us was what I had been missing. I'd been missing someone who cared about what was in my mind and heart. I'd been missing his love and his touch and his arms and his smile and his voice long before I ever knew God had created him, long before he walked into my life and made my heart beat with more of a purpose than it ever had. I loved this man. No matter how short the time we'd known each other was, I loved him with everything in my heart and soul.

Beckton, Arkansas, felt a million miles away. Home for me was wherever Malachi Douglass was.

I watched him smile at the waitress and then let my eyes sweep over the room. People at some of the other tables were staring at him, a few pointed, others whipped out their smart phones and snapped pictures of him, but to know him, one would never believe he was famous. My brother had more of an ego than Malachi did.

He reached across the table for my hand and flashed that trillion-dollar smile at me. "What're you thinking about?"

I met his gaze and matched his smile. "You, and how much I love you, how thankful I am for you, how happy you make me."

He raised both eyebrows and leaned back in his seat a little. "Really? I got it like that?"

I nodded. "You got it like more than that. I really do love you, Malachi."

He stood from his chair and walked around the table, bending over and kissing me tenderly on the lips. "I love you, too, baby."

eighteen
"Love"

Malachi clutched my hand as we made our way to Al's and Davina's front door. With the gift bag in my other hand, I felt nervous, but nowhere near as nervous as the first time I was there. I'd been living with and experiencing life with Malachi for two months by then, and at the very least, I was comfortable with him and confident in what we shared. I was doubtless of his love for me, and that alone boosted my confidence. As we entered their massive living room, my eyes took in the scene before me—cute shower decorations adorning the walls, and white folding chairs holding many of the other football wives and girlfriends were arranged in a semi-circle facing Davina, who sat in a white wing chair with her feet resting on a matching ottoman. She was glowing, but at the same time, looked exhausted, as if she couldn't wait to have that baby.

When she saw me and Malachi walking toward her, she moved to stand, but I stopped her. "No, you stay there. You don't have to get up for me."

"Well, you're gonna have to bend down here and hug me, then. Long time no see! Malachi is gonna have to stop being so selfish with you."

I hugged her with a big grin on my face, and once I backed out of our embrace, she said, "Grab one of those chairs and come sit by me."

I moved to do just that, but Malachi beat me to it, setting the chair down and bending over to kiss my cheek once I was seated.

"Ladies only, Malachi. Al is in his mancave. Take this gift from Maria and put it on the table, then go find him."

Malachi hesitated, his eyes on me.

"Your woman will be fine. She's gonna sit right here with me and help me open these gifts since my sister has disappeared on me. Probably raiding my closet. Go on, Malachi."

This time, he squatted in front of me, resting his hands on my thighs. I leaned forward and kissed him. "Go on. I'll be fine. Love you."

He gave me a smile. "I love you, too. If you need me, text me."

I nodded and watched as he left the room. When I shifted my focus to my immediate surroundings, all eyes were on me, so I said, "Hey, everyone."

Davina muttered, "Girl, he's got it bad. Never seen him like that before, and I've known Malachi for at least five years. Woo wee!"

I giggled lightly. "I've got it bad, too."

"I can tell. Hmm, I wanna be the one to throw you a bridal shower."

"He hasn't even proposed."

"Oh, he will. I guarantee it. And let me tell you now, it's not an easy life being an NFL wife. It can be lonely and especially hard after you start having kids and can't be on the road with your man as much, but I got your back, and Malachi is a great man, a man of God. You just can't get any better than him."

I smiled. "I know. It's a blessing that we found each other."

"I know that's right, girl."

***

The shower was really nice, and Davina loved my gift. Several of the other ladies were shocked when I revealed that I'd sewn the outfits. A woman I remembered meeting at Davina's other party swore they were exact replicas of outfits she'd seen in an upscale boutique.

After the gift opening and accompanying oohing and ahhing, all the ladies took pictures together, and Davina was glowing with excitement over the mountain of expensive gifts she'd received for the little girl they planned to name Alana, matching her siblings' names—Alisha, Al Jr., and Alex.

I was ready to mark this down as one of the best days I'd ever had besides the days I spent with Malachi. Nothing could beat being with him. But just as that triumphant thought entered my mind, I was approached by a tall, statuesque black woman I'd never met before, although she looked vaguely familiar. As a matter of fact, I hadn't even noticed her at the shower up until that point.

As I ladled more of the pink punch into my cup, she stepped up beside me and extended her hand, "Hi, I don't think we've met. I'm Candice."

I turned to face her. She was pretty in an overly made-up, trying too hard to be pretty kind of way. Her curves matched mine, albeit she was much thinner than me, but going strictly by body type, I could see that she possessed the attributes Malachi liked.

I set the cup down and took her hand. "Hi, Candice. I'm Maria. Nice to meet you."

She smiled. "My, what an accent. You're from deep in the south, huh?"

"We're standing deep in the south. We're in Texas." If she thought she was going to make me feel bad about being country or anything else, she was sadly mistaken and a few weeks too late. I'd shed the self-consciousness. Love had made me a new woman.

"Hmm, I suppose so. Well, it's nice to finally meet you in person and not splashed all over Instagram."

"Yes, well…thanks." I grabbed my cup and turned to leave her at the table, but she wasn't done.

"I'm going to get him back, you know? So, don't get too comfortable," she said to my back.

I turned and glanced at her. "I'll keep that in mind."

When I returned to my seat, Davina leaned in, and asked, "You okay? I didn't invite her. I think she snuck in here behind one of these other chicks. Want me to make her leave?"

I shook my head. "I'm fine. She's not bothering me." And she really wasn't. Maybe if she was referring to another man, any man besides Malachi, I would've been shaken. But I knew if she and I were in the same room with him, she was going to be the one to end up with hurt feelings.

My little conversation was scarcely over when I felt a pair of hands on my shoulders. I tilted my head back to see Malachi hovering over me, gazing down at me with a grin on his face.

"Davina," he said. "I'm taking my woman home. You've held her hostage long enough."

"Mm-hmm. You're just selfish," she responded to him, then looked at me, and said, "Maria, make sure to come back and see me, and feel free to make my baby some more dresses."

I smiled as she leaned in and kissed my cheek. "I sure will."

Taking Malachi's hand, I waved goodbye to the other ladies as he released my hand, draped an arm over my shoulders, and kissed me. "Missed you."

"Mm, missed you, too."

We were almost to the front door when her voice rang out in the foyer. "Malachi!"

He stopped in his tracks, glanced at me, and wore a frown as he dropped his arm from my shoulders and turned around.

I kind of just stood there until he reached back and grabbed my hand, pulling me close to him.

"What's up, Candice? You met Maria yet?"

Her eyes narrowed a bit. "Yes, I have. And what's up is *you*, baby. So when you wanna hook up so you can get another taste of this candy I got waiting for you?"

Malachi looked from the right to the left. "Are you talking to me?"

"Of course, silly! Who else?" She moved closer, tried to touch his chest, but he backed out of her reach.

"You do know I'm with Maria now, right? I know someone in there already told you. So you need to chill and stop disrespecting my girl."

Her mouth dropped open. "You're really with her? *Her?* Seriously, Malachi? How do you go from this to that?"

He turned to me with a smile and kissed me so deeply I almost passed out, actually did stumble a bit. "Because this right here?" Malachi said, as he pulled me to him, reached around, and grabbed my butt. "Is so much better than you ever were. I love this woman, Candice, so you should move on. Find another victim, because ain't nothing gonna come of you trying to get with me."

With that, he led me out of the house to his car. "I'm sorry for grabbing your booty like that, baby."

I lifted an eyebrow as I leaned across the center console and kissed him. "Don't be."

He grinned and started the car. If it was possible, I think I fell even more in love with him that day.

nineteen
"Fly Like a Bird"

"Yes!" Malachi yelled, jumping up from the sofa in his living room. We were playing Patton NFL '17 on his Xbox, and he'd just eviscerated me, as usual.

I looked up at him, game controller still in hand. "You know what? You said playing this game was going to help me understand football, but I think you just like beating me."

He fell back on the couch beside me with a grin on his face. "Maria, you know better than that. I love you, baby." He kissed me and I gave him a smirk, my eyes on his lips.

"If you love me, you'll let me win."

"Okay. The next time we play, I'ma let you beat me by like fifty points. But if I do that, what do I get in return?"

"A big old thank you."

"No kiss or hug or booty grab? Nothing?"

I sighed. "Okay, a booty grab and a kiss on the cheek."

"I'll take it! Hey, we need to get ready if we're going to that place I told you about."

We were going to some club some team member had told Malachi about that was supposed to have a laid-back vibe to it, and we were going to be in a private VIP section. No fans. Just us. I hadn't been to anything even resembling a club since Two's, and before that, I had never set foot in any club, so I was excited to get to dress up and dance a little with Malachi. I'd learned to enjoy looking nice since I'd been staying with him. That was something I'd never cared about before, unless I was going to church. I guess I never had time to care about it.

We had a light dinner at a little Italian restaurant before heading to the club around ten that night. The place was huge with a line a mile long at the door.

"Wow," I said, as Malachi opened my door and helped me out of his car. "Look at that line."

"Yeah, don't worry about it, though," he said, as he leaned in and kissed me. "Baby, baby…damn, you look good!"

I grinned, and said, "Thank you," as I took his hand and let him lead me to the building with a neon sign attached to the outside of it that brightly declared we were about to enter Paradise.

I'd opted to wear a sheer red blouse with a black bandeau underneath paired with a black pencil skirt that fell a couple of inches above my knees, fit my wide hips and booty like a glove, and boasted a high split at the left thigh. It was an outfit Malachi had picked out during one of our shopping excursions, telling me that was how he saw me—bold and sexy. My hair was in a big, messy afro, and I'd managed to apply eyeliner, mascara, and a little foundation along with my tinted lip gloss. Malachi was as close to drooling as I'd ever seen him when I stepped into the living room and announced I was ready to go earlier that evening.

He walked past the line with me in tow as people yelled his name and pulled out their phones to take pictures, and when we got to the front of the line, he merely looked at the bouncer who moved to the side to let us by. He didn't even have to pay for us to get into the club! Now that blew my mind. I mean, what kind of sense did it make for them to let a rich man in for free?

Nevertheless, I followed him through the crowded building as he dapped up several guys, smiled and nodded at others, and finally, we arrived in a room upstairs that had a view of the entire dancefloor and stage. There was a sofa, a huge round coffee table, and a fully-stocked bar in the room. My feet were already killing me in the heels I wasn't accustomed to wearing, so I collapsed onto the couch while Malachi headed to the bar.

"It's just us two in here, right?" I asked. "Or is someone else coming? One of your teammates?"

As he handed me a glass of what I supposed was wine, he said, "Just us. No fans, no folks taking pictures with their phones, no teammates. Just me and the woman I love." He sat next to me with a shot glass full of something that definitely wasn't wine and kissed me softly on the lips. "We gon' dance and have a good old time up in here. Just me and my pretty Maria."

I giggled as this time, he leaned in and nuzzled my neck.

He lifted his shot glass. "To us, Maria Brown."

"To us." I took a sip of my wine and actually kind of liked it. I had drunk enough of it at the various restaurants Malachi took me to, to have developed an appreciation for it. The first time I tried it, I had to fight not to frown.

A Bruno Mars song came on and Malachi set his glass on the table, reaching for my hand. "This is the jam! We gotta dance to this!"

I shook my head. "I can't in these shoes. My feet are yelling at me."

"Take 'em off! Come on, baby!"

I gazed up at him grinning down at me looking like something out of my dreams, in a white shirt and black slacks. Pulling my shoes off, I took his hand, and we danced and laughed until we were both exhausted. Then we rested, had something to drink, and danced some more. I had never had so much fun in all my life, and when he pulled me into his arms and we swayed to a slow song, I looked into his eyes, and said, "I love you, 'Chi."

He stopped dancing, held my face in his hands, and said, "I love you, too, baby."

twenty
"Good and Bad"

"Baby, come here!" Malachi called from the living room.

I was sitting at the kitchen table doodling in the sketch pad he'd bought me a couple of days earlier, trying to think of something other than him to draw. "What is it?!" I called back, as if I wasn't going to go in there. I actually missed him, was just trying to make myself not be up under him all the time.

"We're on TV!"

"What?" I said, as I made my way to him.

Sitting back on the couch with his feet propped up on the coffee table, he pointed to an image of him and me frozen on the screen. "Let me rewind it."

I sat down next to him, feeling him shift his body so that it was touching mine, and smiled. I loved when he did that.

"Here we go." He pressed play on the DVR remote and I watched us holding hands, leaving the hospital after visiting with Davina and Al and delivering another gift for their gorgeous new baby. I'd gotten to hold her and had experienced an overwhelming desire to have one of my own. By Malachi.

"Al Hegemon's teammates were out in force to offer their support to his growing family, including one of the Cowboys' shining stars, Malachi Douglass, and the mystery woman who's been seen on his arm several times recently. That's right. It looks like one of the team's most eligible bachelors might be off the market soon. Sources tell us a proposal is right around the corner," the *Entertainment Times* correspondent said.

He paused the TV again, and I turned and stared at him with a frown on my face. "Proposal? What source are they talking about?"

He shrugged. "I have no idea. I haven't discussed us or my future plans for us with anyone."

"Future plans that include a proposal?"

"Maria, I told you what my intentions were a long time ago. You know I love you and eventually want to make you my wife. I guess whoever said whatever can see how I feel about you. I don't know. But look, there's always gonna be someone saying something and pictures taken because of who I am and what I do."

"I've noticed."

"You okay with that?"

I sighed. "I love you, so I guess I'll *have* to be okay with it."

"You sure?"

"Are you going to quit playing football if I'm not sure?"

He rested his hand on my thigh. "You want me to quit?"

"I want you to do what makes you happy."

"You're what makes me happy. Football is a close second."

I smiled as he leaned in to kiss me. "You make me happy, too."

***

When I first heard my phone buzzing on the nightstand, I thought it was just more people from back home texting or leaving voicemails about seeing me on TV, since I'd been getting a ton of those. People from Brown Boy's, people from church, random people I really didn't know and had no idea how they'd gotten my number. There was even a message from some entertainment blogger. So I ignored the buzzing until I realized it wasn't stopping. Malachi was fast asleep, but I couldn't sleep with the noise so close to my side of the bed and decided to just shut my phone off altogether. But once it was in my hand and I saw that instead of messages, there was a string of missed calls on my screen, all from Spring, I panicked. It would've been one thing for Felton to call, but for Spring to call me and in the middle of the night? Something must've been terribly wrong.

I eased out from under the arm Malachi had flung across my waist and quietly left his bed, closing myself in his bathroom where I dialed my sister-in-law's number. I took a seat on the toilet as the phone rang in my ear.

No answer.

I was so anxious, I just hung up without leaving a message and redialed her number. This time she answered. "Hello? Maria?"

"Spring? What's going on? Why are you calling so late?" I asked in a hushed voice.

"Because…I had to find a time to call when Felton wouldn't hear me. Look, your brother is angry with you because you haven't been returning his calls, so he's not going to tell you this, but your parents are having surgery in the morning."

"What? *Both* of them?"

"Yeah. Your mom is giving your father a kidney. It was a miracle that she was a match."

"What?!" I had raised my voice, but I couldn't help it.

"Yeah, so you really should come home. I mean, they're both going under the knife. You never know what could happen, Maria. If something goes wrong, you don't want that guilt on your shoulders."

I held the phone, several emotions plaguing me at the same time.

"Sis, just think about it. If you decide to come, they go into surgery at six in the morning. I hope to see you at the hospital. We'll be in the surgery waiting area."

"Um, okay. Thanks for letting me know."

"Yeah, and hey, I saw you on TV. You look so good, Maria. And if you do decide to come home, make sure you take yourself right back to that man. He's good for you."

I smiled. "He is. Thanks."

I opened the bathroom door and walked into the bedroom to find the lights on and Malachi missing from the bed. I kind of just stood there and stared at the empty bed, because if I ever needed him, I did at that moment. As I started for the door to find him, he entered the room, adjusting the waist of his pajama bottoms. Seeing the look on my face, he said, "I guess we had to go at the same time."

I fell into him, holding him tight.

"Hey, you all right?" he asked.

"No, you were gone." It didn't make any sense for me to be this upset, and I knew he probably thought I'd lost my mind, but he also didn't know about the news I'd just received or how torn I was at that moment. The last thing I wanted to do was leave him and what he provided for me—love, peace, security—things my family had largely neglected to give me.

He backed away a bit and cupped my face in his hands. "Baby, what's wrong?"

I lifted my phone. "I just got a call…"

He frowned. "Someone bothering you? About us?"

I shook my head and stepped away from him, sitting on the side of his bed. "My sister-in-law." I gave him the news, ending with my mixed feelings about going home, although I knew that was what I needed to do.

He sat beside me. "Are you worried about going home because of your mother being there or because you're afraid something will change between us?"

"I don't wanna leave you."

"I'll go with you."

"But training camp—"

"Starts next week. I'll stay there with you as long as I can, and once they're both out of the woods, I'll send for you. Nothing's going to change between us. I love you now, I'll love you tomorrow, I'll always love you."

He wrapped his arms around me and I leaned into him. "I love you, too."

twenty-one
"Never Let Go"

I'm sure I was squeezing the life out of Malachi's hand as we navigated our way through the hospital to the surgery waiting room, but he didn't complain or try to free his hand from mine. I was a bundle of tangled, disorganized nerves on the way to the airport, on the plane, in the rental car to Beckton, and now, in the confines of the cold hospital, I feared I would completely lose it. There, in that town, the memories and emotions that plagued me for most of my life, but had dulled and lost their edge during my time in Dallas, hovered over me, blocking the light Malachi had bathed me in. I just felt…heavy, like I was carrying extra weight akin to the physical weight of an eighteen-wheeler.

As we approached the familiar faces of Felton, Spring, my father's friend, Mr. Thomas, and two women I recognized as my mother's sisters only because of how closely they resembled her and me, I felt something slam into my chest and just sit there, compressing my heart and lungs, making it nearly impossible to breathe.

I turned to Malachi, slapping my hand against my chest and shaking my head.

He dropped my hand and grasped my arms. "What is it? What is it, baby?"

"I…I can't do this. Take me back. Take me back *now*."

I couldn't control the volume of my voice or my breathing or the wild shaking of my hands. I closed my eyes, heard voices around me, felt someone I prayed was Malachi leading me somewhere…to a chair. I sat, bent forward and buried my face in my hands, heard people talking, too many voices to really make out what was being said, until I heard, "I've got her. I've got her. Just let me help her. No…you can go sit down."

Malachi.

And then, I felt his warm breath skim my ear as he whispered, "Breathe. Just breathe, baby. I'm right here. I'm not leaving you. You're okay, but you've got to breathe."

So I breathed, leaning against him, my eyes still closed. I was sure all eyes were on me, but if I was going to make it through whatever this was, I couldn't and wouldn't care about how any of it looked.

I breathed, felt him grasp my hand, kiss my cheek, wipe my tears away, tell me he loved me, pray softly into my ear, and I was okay again.

I opened my eyes to see Felton staring at me, but I couldn't read his face. It wasn't a look of concern or love or…I couldn't tell what he was thinking, but it didn't feel like anything good. And that made me want to run from that hospital even more, but Daddy was in surgery. So was my mother. It was the decent and right thing to be there.

But decent and right for who? Them? Me? The people in the community who would think ill of me had I not come back? Why was I there?

"Hey, you okay now?" Spring asked, sliding into the seat adjoined to the right side of mine. Malachi was on my left, still holding my hand.

I nodded. "I'm better, as okay as I'm going to get right now."

"I know you're worried. We all are, but this will really be a blessing once they've both recovered. It'll truly be a new start for them as newlyweds again."

I just stared at Spring. If she and Felton talked at all, and I happened to be privy to the fact that they did, she knew my parents' remarriage wasn't something that brought me joy.

Seeing the expression on my face, or perhaps filling my deliberate silence with my unspoken thoughts, she patted my knee, and said, "Well, I'm just glad you made it back safely. You look fabulous, by the way," and then left to reclaim her seat by Felton.

My aunts looked at me and nodded, and I was thankful they didn't try to talk to me or act like they knew me. Daddy's friend gave me a reassuring smile. And then it was Felton's turn to take the seat next to mine.

"You feeling better?" he asked, his eyes on the floor rather than my face.

"Yeah. I'm...how long they been back there?"

"A little over an hour. Since Spring called and told you about this last night, I thought you'd at least try to get here before they took them back for surgery. It would've been nice if Daddy could've seen you this morning since you're all he talks about." There was a definite edge to his hushed voice, like he was more than a little perturbed at me.

I glanced at Malachi, who had his eyes fixed on the TV hanging on the wall a few feet in front of us. It was tuned to ESPN. "Uh, we got here as early as we could."

Well, that was a lie. I actually backed out of coming back that morning, and we missed our first flight because it took a couple of hours for Malachi to coax me into the car. He even had to pack my bag, because I refused to.

Felton nodded. "Yeah. Look, Maria. You're going to have to get yourself together. Mama and Daddy are the ones who need everyone's attention. Not you. Don't pull another one of those little stunts again."

He left before I could respond, and I had to wonder what in the world was going on. Felton had been a lot of things, distant, invalidating, even selfish, but downright mean? That had never been him. What had changed in the time I was gone?

I frowned, and the longer I sat there, the more I confirmed to myself that being there was a mistake. But I was there, Malachi was, too, had paid for plane tickets. So I didn't move from that seat for the next two hours. I also didn't let his hand go.

"You okay?" he must've asked a thousand times. He obviously hadn't heard my little exchange with Felton, and I honestly didn't even know how to explain what had happened between us to him, so I nodded and replied with, "As long as you're here, I am."

He smiled. "Then you're going to stay okay. I'm not leaving you."

When a doctor finally emerged and called for the Brown family, I didn't and couldn't move, no matter how much encouragement Malachi gave me. By then I was hungry and had to pee, but I knew if I stood for any reason, I was going to end up leaving. It turned out I could hear him from where I sat anyway. They were both fine. The surgery had gone off without a hitch. Now all there was left to do was to wait and see if Daddy's new kidney would begin making urine. Despite my internal turmoil, I breathed a sigh of relief, thanked God, and felt myself relax a bit. And I finally went to the restroom and grabbed a bite to eat before we were allowed to visit them.

***

In his room hours later, Daddy didn't look like himself, and by that I mean he looked good, better. His skin looked clearer than it had in years, he'd gained some weight, and when he saw me, wore an unfamiliar smile. Daddy hadn't smiled like that in ages, and I knew these changes had nothing to do with his new kidney. They had everything to do with my mother. In the short amount of time she'd spent back in Beckton with him, she'd been able to do what I'd failed to do over the years, she'd made Daddy happy. Love had made him happy. I knew the side effects of love well, because I'd experienced them with Malachi and realized as Daddy looked at me, he probably saw similar changes in me.

"Hey, 'Ria," he said, stretching a hand toward me.

I was in the room alone, and as good as he looked, as long as I had prayed to see these changes in him, I wasn't happy for him. I was angry, because my years of sacrifice hadn't brought the same result. So I didn't take his hand. Instead, I stood next to his bed and averted my gaze to the window in his room.

He lowered his hand. "I know you're angry about me and your mother. Probably feel betrayed after all me and you been through over the years since she left."

Surprised, I lifted an eyebrow and fixed my eyes on him again. Daddy had never acknowledged what we'd gone through because of her actions. Me and him just lived it day by day. Never discussed it at all.

"But she's different now. Settled. And she's good for me. Gave me a new life with this kidney."

I nodded. "Well, good for you, Daddy," was all I could think to say.

Silence, and then he said, "You look good. That boy been treating you right out there in Dallas?"

"Better than right."

"You love him?"

"Very much."

"Wouldn't want to lose him then, huh?"

I shook my head. I knew where he was going with this. "Never."

"And if he left, and then came back to you, would you take him back?"

"I don't know, Daddy. It would depend on the circumstances."

"What if the circumstances were him begging you to do more than work and go to church and stay at home? What if you'd been neglecting his needs, not giving him support when he needed it, or at least not the kind he needed. What if he pleaded with you to move somewhere else, to explore the world with him, and even though you knew that was something he needed, you refused because you were afraid? What if him leaving was your fault, because you just wouldn't listen or try to see things his way?"

I grasped the bed railing. "Is that what you think? Is that what you've been telling yourself all these years? Is that why you almost drank yourself to death, *literally*? Because you think it was all your fault? So it was your fault she chose to have an affair, too? Or was that *my* fault since it was my boyfriend she left with and you've decided she's not responsible for her own actions?"

"I didn't say that. I'm saying there are two sides to everything, Maria, and you never saw the whole picture of what happened between me and your mother. That's my fault, and now I'm taking responsibility for my part in this. I knew how she was. I knew how…restless she could get, and I didn't heed that. Keeping her in this town, in a little box of a life, was suffocating her and I knew it, could see it, but instead of doing something about it, I just hoped she'd stay when I knew she'd eventually leave. You can't ask a person to be someone other than themselves forever. That's like slowly killing them."

He winced and I frowned. "You need me to call a nurse?" I asked.

"No, I just need you to forgive her. She's sorry, Maria. And she regrets hurting you more than anything. I think she'd give her life for your forgiveness."

My eyes found their way to the window again.

"Just think about it. And go see her. Check on her for me."

I sighed.

"Please."

"Felton's in there with her now. He can tell you how she's doing."

"But I want you to."

I closed my eyes. "Fine, Daddy. I'll go see her."

He smiled again. "Thank you. And let me say this: I'm sorry, Maria. It was wrong of me to hold you back all those years. You deserved better than what you were forced to deal with, and it was selfish of me to keep you here."

"Daddy, you didn't keep me here. I wanted to stay and take care of you."

"I know, but I should've insisted you leave. I should've guided you like a father is supposed to do. But you've got Malachi now, and I can tell he's good for you."

I nodded. "He is."

"And he makes you happy?"

"He really does."

"Then he gets my approval, not that he needs it."

"I appreciate that, Daddy. I really do."

twenty-two
"Try"

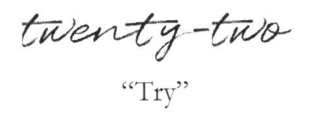

I didn't go see my mother that first day after surgery, or the next day. On the third day, Malachi talked me into it, even promised to go in there with me.

When we entered the room, she was sitting up in bed talking on her cell phone. The procedure to remove her kidney was a less invasive one than Daddy's, as they were able to do it laparoscopically, so her recovery seemed a little more rapid than his.

Her entire face lit up when I entered the room, and she quickly ended her phone call. A childish little part of me, a part that was stuck back in high school and kept reliving the night she left, wondered if it was Terrance on the other end, but I didn't voice that thought.

"Maria!" she nearly shouted, stopping me in my tracks near the door. I still wasn't ready for this. What was I supposed to say to her? I didn't even know how to greet her. Was I supposed to call her Mama like I used to? Well, I couldn't do that. She had ceased being my mother long ago.

Malachi released my hand and stepped forward, proffering one of his hands to her. As he introduced himself, and they exchanged some kind words, I let my eyes drift to the TV. She still watched *The Young and the Restless.*

"...Maria?"

I frowned slightly and turned to see Malachi looking at me expectantly.

"Huh-what?"

"I'm gonna go grab some coffee. Want some?"

My eyes pleaded with him not to leave me with her. In return, he gave me a smile and leaned in close, kissing my cheek and whispering, "I'll be right back," before leaving me standing there.

A few seconds later, my mother said, "Why don't you sit down, sweetie?"

Sweetie.

I fell into the chair next to her bed, the only one in her room, and stared at the TV as if I cared about what was happening on it.

After three or four minutes of thick silence, she said, "I need to say something to you. I know you don't want to hear it, but I need for you to just listen to me."

I didn't reply or shift my gaze from the TV.

"I know you hate me, and if I were you, I'd hate me, too. I can't imagine what it would feel like if my mother did to me what I did to you. I can't imagine what it's been like watching Senior fall apart."

Senior. I'd forgotten she called Daddy that.

"But I want you to believe me when I tell you I've spent all these years hating myself more than you could ever hate me. I lost my family, my precious daughter, because of what I did. I broke my own heart when I left."

I shrugged. "You had Felton. He's always been on your side."

"Junior has kept in touch with me, yes, but do you think I haven't wanted you in my life, too? You think I just left and never turned back, and that's not the case. Do you think a day has gone by that I didn't want to see you or talk to you? Most of me and your brother's conversations were about you and your father, but especially you."

I shook my head.

"They were! I was worried about how you were living your life."

"I *wasn't* living! I didn't *have* a life! I was doing your damn job, taking care of the husband you dumped!" I screamed.

She jumped a little. I couldn't blame her. I actually startled myself. It seemed as if all the emotions I had been suppressing over the years, especially my anger, decided to jump out at her at that moment.

"I have *never* had a life! My so-called life has been to clean up *your* mess! To-to be the responsible one when you wouldn't! You don't get it at all, do you? How completely miserable an existence I lived after you left. The day you walked out the door with my boyfriend, I stopped being a teenager and became a grown woman, a nurse, a-an old lonely person with no life. You took my life and left me behind to live yours!"

I looked at her, saw the tears racing down her face, but didn't care.

"*You* took vows with Daddy, not me. But who stuck around and helplessly watched him suffer? I did! Who tried to help him? I did! And when I finally find some happiness, when I finally have a good life, I'm expected to come back here and act like you and him getting back together is just a dream come true for me after all these years? Well, the truth is I'm tired! I'm done with you and him and everyone else expecting anything from me!"

I left, running into Malachi in the hallway, tears filling my eyes. A few minutes later, we were on our way to my house.

***

"No. I can't do it." I shook my head to emphasize my refusal.

"Look, it's just temporary. Just for a couple of weeks until they can take care of themselves," Felton said.

"Get them an aide."

"They're going to send someone to help them with their baths, but that's only for a couple of hours a day. They'll need 'round the clock help."

"You and Spring can move in with them, then. I did my time."

"That's how you're going to refer to taking care of our father? Really?"

I sighed. "That's what it felt like. Of course you wouldn't understand, though, would you?"

He leaned back in the chair in my living room. "Maria, I've got a lot going on at the church. I can't be there all day, and Spring has her job. It's only for a couple of weeks. And Malachi is leaving for training camp in a couple of days, right? So you'd be in Dallas alone anyway."

"I know people in Dallas. Malachi made sure of that. I won't be alone, because I can visit them," I countered, thinking mostly of Davina.

Malachi was quietly sitting next to me, but I knew he wanted me to stay, because it was supposedly the right thing to do. I was over sacrificing my happiness to do the right thing.

"Maria, come on. Don't do this. They need you. And like I said, it's just temporary."

I folded my arms over my chest.

"Um, can you give us a minute?" Malachi said, and I let my arms fall from my chest. There was no sense in Felton leaving or Malachi talking to me, because I already knew I was going to give in to him. He knew it, too, so I said, "Two weeks. I'll stay two weeks. No more."

Felton breathed a sigh of relief.

Malachi smiled at me. "I'll get you a ticket to fly back to Dallas dated for two weeks from today."

As he leaned in to kiss my cheek, I said, "You better."

twenty-three
"Supposed to Be"

Two weeks turned into three, then four, and eventually, several weeks passed and I was still in Beckton.

It wasn't that anything went wrong. Daddy's new kidney was functioning well, my mother was healing rapidly, and so was Daddy, but there was so much to take care of—follow-up appointments, managing Daddy's new medication regimen with the added anti-rejection pills, making sure they ate and drank the right things, especially with Daddy being a diabetic, but I was pleased to see he was now willing to adhere to his diet, hadn't gone near any alcohol, and was thrilled to have this new lease on life.

Somehow, I fell back into life in Beckton pretty easily. I suppose familiarity is always easy to slip back into. I would take care of them without really acknowledging or speaking to my mother, but caring for her nonetheless. I would go to church, and I even visited the old crew at Brown Boy's from time to time, laughing at their ridiculous requests for autographs from me. Malachi left a couple of days after I agreed to stay, and although I missed him terribly, there were times when him and Dallas seemed a million years in my past. That life, life with him, almost felt like something I'd dreamed up. Being in Beckton, cooking and washing clothes and sitting alone in my childhood bedroom, was, and always had been, my reality. And so was the heavy sadness that accompanied it.

I hated being there, but there was a part of me that felt comfortable in the normalcy of that misery. I spoke to Malachi on the phone, put on a good act of pretending to be fine, but I wasn't, and had dug in so deep that I didn't know how to pull myself back out. I needed him, but he couldn't save me this time. He had a job to do. So I stayed and helped, and little by little, lost the person I became when I was with him, until I could actually feel myself begin to disappear.

***

"Welcome to Brown Boy's, how can I help you?"

The couple quickly rattled off their order, and I stuck the ticket on the carousel for the kitchen crew to fill it. It was a busy Saturday afternoon, and my feet were killing me.

"Maria, you going to the game on Monday?" the man at the counter, a member of my church, asked.

I knew he was referring to the Cowboys' season opener in Texas, and as badly as I didn't want to think about that, I said, "No. I'm helping out with the food pantry at church all day Monday."

He gave me this odd look, as if I didn't know how ridiculous I sounded. My man was playing a game, an *NFL* game, and I wasn't even attempting to go and support him. Well, I guessed he was still my man, but maybe not since I'd been ignoring his phone calls for an entire week. I just couldn't talk to him, because I knew he was expecting me to come back, and that was something I wasn't sure I could do. And I honestly had no idea why. It was like something in Beckton had a hold on me and wouldn't let me go.

I finished the man's transaction and yelled into the kitchen that I was heading outside for some air. I stood on the sidewalk and tried not to cry. Was leaning against the brick wall next to the door when she pulled up, climbing out of an old minivan and hobbling toward me on her cane with something between a smile and a frown on her face.

"Ms. Two?" I said.

"Uh-huh."

"You…what can I do for you? Come on inside."

"I didn't come here for barbecue. I came here on behalf of my Malachi."

His grandmother had called me a few days earlier and made small talk. I'd thought he asked her to call, but she never brought him up and now Ms. Two? "He asked you to come here?"

"No. He wouldn't impose on me like that. He knows I'm old as hell, too old to be driving up here."

I smiled a little.

"What's going on between you and my boy? I talked to him earlier today, called him like I do before the start of every season to pray with him over the phone, and he sounds miserable, says you won't even talk to him and he doesn't know why. He thinks you got another guy."

"No! I-I love Malachi. I wouldn't do that!"

"Then why are you still in town, working here like that boy wouldn't move Heaven and Earth to take care of you? You're all he talks about, and he's stressed out with them losing half of their pre-season games. Says he can't concentrate with you shutting him out."

"I didn't mean to hurt him. Truthfully, I don't know why I'm here or what I'm doing…"

"Well, you need to figure it out. I know love when I see it. I saw it between you two at my club that night. I heard it in his voice along with a lot of confusion. And I see it right now, behind those tears in your eyes. He said he regretted encouraging you to stay, that he believes this place is holding on to you and won't let you go. I agree with him. I can feel it. Look, honey, I don't know what it is, if you have some unfinished business holding you in this little town away from a man who absolutely adores you or what, but if there is, you need to straighten it out, and you need to do it now!"

twenty-four
"Stand"

I knew what I needed to do. I needed to leave, to go to Malachi, but for the life of me, I just couldn't. I was paralyzed, couldn't even call him, and by then, he had stopped calling me. I didn't sleep that night after Ms. Two's visit, her words infiltrating my mind every time I closed my eyes. She was right. There was some unfinished business I needed to attend to. And the more I thought about it, I was sure both my inability to leave and my lack of peace in not leaving was the work of God. There was something He wanted me to do, and until I did it, I would never feel right.

That Sunday morning before church, I knocked on the door to Felton's study and entered when he yelled, "Come in!" He looked handsome in his black suit as he sat poring over his sermon notes.

He glanced up at me, and seeing my attire, fixed his eyes on me as I stood in front of his desk, a look of displeasure shadowing his face. "I know you're not wearing that to church. Jeans and a t-shirt?"

"No, I'm not. I'm not attending church today. I'm leaving, going back to Dallas."

He reclined in his high-backed chair and sighed. "Back to that again, huh? You're just going to abandon your family to chase after some ball player?"

I frowned. "What?"

"You belong here, Maria. In this town, in this church, at home with Mama and Daddy, not in Dallas with him, running all over town in those little dresses he bought you, taking pictures with *his* fans. You looked ridiculous. That life is not for you."

I almost wanted to look around to see if I was in some sort of alternate reality. What had gotten into him? "But you and Spring were the ones who put me in front of him. You and him are friends, right? You told him all my business and everything. I thought you *wanted* me to be with him."

"Not anymore! I mean, he seems nice and all, but can't you see he's using you?"

"Using me for what? What could he possibly be using my uneducated, country behind for, Felton?"

"Sex, Maria," he said, lowering his voice. "That's what all men use women for. Even *I* did back in the day. You need to get whatever fantasy he's been selling you out of your head."

"Huh? Where in the world is this coming from?"

"It's coming from the fact that I can see he doesn't really care about you. He can't!"

"Can't? Why? Because you think all I'm good for is being here doing what you don't want to do, man of God? Huh? Because you're too good to get your hands dirty and take care of your own parents? I'm supposed to do the scut work, have absolutely no life? Me and only me, while you sit up in here in your suits and serve the people from your ivory tower?!"

"Keep your voice down."

"No! I don't care what the folks in this church think about me, and I don't care what *you* think, either. You were fine with Malachi until I went to Dallas and stayed and you were left to deal with Daddy and Mama and whatever. Well, I told you two weeks, stayed for seven, *seven*, but I'm leaving now. I'm going back home."

"This is your home. Beckton is your home!"

"Not anymore! And don't worry, our mother has basically fully recovered and can help Daddy. You don't have to do anything for them since you haven't even bothered to visit since I've been back, you fake preacher. Visiting the sick and the shut-in and won't even visit your own parents!"

"That is not my job!"

"But it's mine?!"

"What else do you have to do with your time, Maria? I mean, you complain about all the years you lost taking care of Daddy—yeah, Mama told me about your little conversation with her in the hospital—but what would you have done otherwise? What did you have going for you? I have a calling on my life, responsibilities that are far more important than anything you could've ever done."

My mouth dropped open. There it was, what he really thought of me, how he really saw me. He'd just opened his mouth and voiced exactly how insignificant he thought my life and feelings were. "You think I didn't have dreams? Are you honestly going to sit there as one who was called by God, who claims to have an intimate relationship with Him, and tell me you think His plan, His *only* plan for me is to be miserable in this little town? That he designed my life only for that? Now I know I was here for a purpose, but I also know it's time for me to leave. And if you can't see that it's destroying me to stay here, if you can't tell how much Malachi and I love each other, then I have no choice but to question if you really do talk to and hear from God."

He stared at me with fire in his eyes, and in that moment, I saw my big brother for what I'd always known him to be, even if he didn't always display it—selfish. Totally and completely selfish.

"How dare you question my spirituality!" he spat.

"How dare you expect me to sacrifice the rest of my life so you can live comfortably with no responsibilities other than to this church! Your first ministry and commitment is to your family. You know how I know that? You said it in one of your own sermons! See, I listened to you, Felton. Did you listen to yourself?"

"Maria—"

"No! I'm leaving, and I don't know when or if I'll ever be back. You don't have to like it, but I'm a grown woman, so there's nothing you can do to stop me. And the only reason I'm telling you is because, as your parents' caregiver, I thought you should know."

"*Our* parents," he corrected.

I nodded. "That's right. That's exactly right, Felton. Not just mine, but *our* parents."

And with that, I left his study and headed to my parents' house to find Malachi sitting in their living room.

twenty-five
"Break Every Chain"

"What...Malachi? You have a game tomorrow. What are you doing here?"

"He says he's come to take you home with him," my father said. I hadn't even noticed him sitting in his easy chair grinning from ear to ear. "I asked him what took him so long," Daddy joked.

I wanted to smile but was too shocked to. So I just stood there and tried not to cry. I had missed him so much.

"Maria, I'm not taking no for an answer. Go get your stuff so we can go," Malachi said.

"Malachi—"

"I don't know what's wrong, but we can work it out. I love you, and if I did or said something—"

"Malachi, I wasn't going to say no. I love you, too, and I'm sorry for... everything. I was actually planning to surprise you by flying to Dallas today. Already have a ticket, and my stuff is packed."

His face lit up. "Really, baby?"

I nodded. "Yeah, *really*. There's something I need to do first, though, something I *have* to do. Can you give me a few minutes?"

He grinned. "As long as you're coming home with me, I'll give you an hour."

"I won't need it." I kissed his cheek and turned to my father. "Daddy, where is…where's M-Mama?"

"In the kitchen. Said she felt good enough to cook, so she'd starting early on dinner. And guess what? We're going to church next Sunday."

I lifted my eyebrows. "Really? That's great, Daddy." And it truly was.

"Hopefully, we'll get to come to Dallas one day and meet Pastor Cloud," Daddy hinted.

Daddy was talking about leaving Beckton? Wow!

"Most definitely!" Malachi said. "Just say the word and I'll personally introduce you to him."

I grabbed Malachi's hand and squeezed it before heading into the kitchen where Mama sat at the table picking greens. She looked up at me and smiled. "Aren't these some nice-looking greens? My sister, Melva, brought them over while you were gone."

I nodded. "I bet they're gonna be good, too. You always made the best greens."

Her lip trembled a little. "It's the seasoning. My mama's recipe. I'll have to give it to you so you can cook some for that good-looking man out there."

I smiled as I sat across from her. "I'd like that. I'm-I'm sorry for being so mean to you."

She shook her head. "No, you had every right to be. Still do."

"And I forgive you."

She looked up at me, stilled her busy hands, and just barely above a whisper, said, "You don't have to. I'll understand if you never forgive me. I don't deserve it. I was selfish and I left you behind for a boy, a child I had no business fooling with. And I am so deeply sorry for that. I just…I don't know. This town was never for me, and I always knew that. Your father did, too. It just closed in on me and snuffed the life out of me."

"I honestly understand. I-I get it, the part where you wanted to leave and Daddy wouldn't. I just don't understand the part with Terrance."

She sighed, dropping her eyes for a moment and then fixing them on me again. "That was…to be honest, he was easy for me to manipulate. He was young, would do anything I said, so I-I used him to get what I wanted. See, I wanted to leave but was afraid to do it alone."

"But why *my* boyfriend? I really cared about him."

"I know you did. Probably more than I did. Maria, sweetie, all I can say is he was there all the time. He was always at the house, and I just needed a way out. He came on to me first. That's not an excuse, but it's the truth. I resisted for a while, and then I just gave in. He had all these dreams of moving away and I latched on to them, saw that boy as my hero, my escape plan. It was wrong, one hundred percent, dead wrong, but I did it. I'll never forgive myself for doing that to you."

"Yeah, I remember him having those dreams. He shared them with me, too."

"Maria, I know none of what I'm saying is what you want to hear. You probably wish I had a valid reason for doing what I did, but I didn't. The truth is, there's no good reason to hurt the people you love, and sometimes people just do bad things. I did a very bad thing, a horrible thing, because of selfishness.

"The best I can tell you is I believed I'd given up the life I really wanted for your father, because I loved him so much. I thought when you and your brother were grown, he'd be willing to leave, and when I saw that wasn't going to happen, I decided to take my life back. But, you were right about what you said in the hospital. I *did* take your life from you. I don't think I did it on purpose or consciously at all, but that's exactly what I did. I saw the freedom you had and I wanted it, so I took it."

I frowned and wanted to look away from her, but was determined to keep my eyes locked on hers. "Well, I hated you for a long time because of it, but I honestly have a better life now. If I'd left with Terrance, if we'd stayed together, if I hadn't stayed here, I never would've met Malachi. I wouldn't give anything for what I have with him."

She smiled. "Isn't it something how God works things out? If I had never left your father, I would've never realized that with him is where I was supposed to be all the time. I don't think I ever would've appreciated him. And if I hadn't come back when I did, I couldn't have helped him."

"What…what happened to you and Terrance?"

She sighed. "Well, we grew apart, I guess. I never thought we were a forever thing, and when he started talking about wanting children a little over a year ago, I knew it was time to end things. I knew I needed to let him go find someone who could do that for him, and I felt like it was time for me to come home. We'd been divorced a few months when Junior called me about your father, and I saw that as a sign that I was right."

I stared at the table and blinked back tears. "He-he wanted kids?"

She nodded. "He did. Probably got him one by now."

I looked up at her again. "There...there was a baby. I—after you left, I found out I was pregnant by Terrance."

Her mouth dropped open as she leaned forward, looking like I'd just slapped her across the face. "Maria, what?"

"I-uh, I found out I was pregnant with Terrance's baby."

"N-no one told me. Not Junior or your father. No one…"

I shook my head as the tears began to fall. "That's because they never knew. I never told anyone until now. You're the only person besides me who knows."

The atmosphere was heavy and silent as my mother stared at me before finally asking, "Where's the baby?"

"I didn't have it," I sobbed. "I took Daddy's car one Saturday morning and went to that doctor you took me to when I first started my period. Paid him for an abortion with some of the money I'd saved up from working at Brown Boy's. He did it right there in his office. Daddy thought I was having female troubles when I stayed in bed the rest of the weekend."

"Maria—"

"I didn't know what else to do. My mother was gone. The father of my baby, the boy I loved, was gone. My father was a wreck. My brother just couldn't be bothered with any of it. And me? I was an emotional mess and barely functioning at that point. I couldn't have taken care of a baby, or at least that's how I saw it at the time. I've regretted it since. I wish I'd made a different choice, but I didn't have anybody to help me work through it. No mother, no father, no boyfriend, and all my friends had turned away from me after news spread about you and Terrance. I guess no one wanted to be around me, because a blind man could see I was depressed. I was...I was all alone, so alone."

Now she was crying, too.

"So...I did it, and I tried to move on, but a little part of me died with that baby, and I just never really healed from it. But right now, telling you about it, I feel ten times lighter. I feel like I can finally move past it. I don't feel like I'm carrying it alone anymore. And I think maybe I can even tell Malachi about it now."

"Maria...oh, sweetie. I am so sorry. I'm so, so sorry."

"Do you know we only did it once? And I haven't done it since. Not even with Malachi."

She swiped at the tears flooding her cheeks. "Sweetheart, I wish I had known. I wish...I wish I'd been a better person. I just—I'm sorry."

I nodded. "I wish a lot of things had been different, too. I wish I'd been stronger."

She reached across the table and grasped my hand tightly in hers. "Maria, you *were* strong. All you went through? Taking care of your father? He told me how bad it was for you. And to now know you were carrying this burden the whole time? Sweetie, you're the strongest person I know."

I wiped my face with my hand. "You really think so?"

"I *know* so."

We sat there in comfortable silence for a few minutes, and then I slipped my hand from hers and stood from the table. "Uh, I have to go."

"Not staying for dinner?"

"No, Malachi's got a game tomorrow and he shouldn't even be here, so we need to get back to Dallas."

She nodded. "Good for you! For a while there, I was afraid you were going to stay here. Not that I wouldn't like to get reacquainted with you, but you don't belong here anymore than I did at your age. You belong with that boy out there."

"I do. Hey, how about this? We can talk on the phone sometimes and get to know each other again."

"I'd love that, and I love you, Maria. You don't have to say it back. I just wanted you to know."

"I love you, too, Mama. I never stopped. That was why things were so hard for me. I never stopped loving you or missing you."

"Me either, sweetie."

I took a deep breath and released it, walked from the kitchen to the living room, and said, "Let me grab my things and we can go, okay?" to Malachi.

As if on cue, he dropped to one knee, thrusting the most gorgeous ring I'd ever seen at me. "Will you marry me?"

Behind me, my mother giggled as she stood in the kitchen doorway. Daddy was grinning like the Cheshire cat, still in his chair, and all I could do was let my tears fall as I whispered, "Yes."

twenty-six
"Addictive Love"

One month later...

"I know you probably wanted us to have a big wedding, and we can still do that later, baby," Malachi said, as we lay in our bedroom in our house in Dallas, having wed at the Dallas County courthouse with Davina, Al, and nearly Malachi's entire family present.

A part of me wished my family had been there, but not enough for it to bother me. I could've taken my vows at a factory in front of a group of assembly line workers and I still would've been happy. I had married the man of my dreams on a beautiful October Wednesday afternoon, my parents were back in Arkansas happy and healthy, and I'd finally lost my virginity, because after what Malachi had just given me, I didn't know what to call that one time with Terrance. A good effort? A nice try? How my mother could've left home for that was beyond me. She had to be truly desperate to get out of Beckton, and that I could understand, but still…

"I never said I wanted a big wedding. You assumed I did," I responded, relaxing against his hard body.

"You sure you're okay with us getting married like this?"

"Yeah, what's done is done. I mean, I used to want Felton to officiate my wedding, but he's still mad at me, so…"

He kissed the top of my head. "He'll come around."

"Maybe, maybe not. Either way, I'll keep praying for him."

"Me, too." He was quiet, and then he said, "We can have a big party back in Beckton after the season is over and invite all your folks. You know, like a reception. Or we could have it here and fly them in."

"Either way, it sounds good to me."

"Speaking of something good…"

I grinned against his chest. "Hmm?"

"Maria Douglass, I just want you to know you were definitely worth the wait."

"Mmm, so were you, and I waited much longer than you did, 'The Cowboys' most eligible bachelor.'"

"You make it sound like I just been throwing my thang all over Dallas or something."

I laughed. "You definitely ain't no virgin, not that I'm complaining."

"Oh, so you liked that?" I could hear the wide smile in his voice.

"Mm-hmm…"

"Want some more of it?"

"Mm-hmm…"

"So why are we talking, then?"

I stretched up and kissed him. "You're the one who started this conversation, not me."

He gently pushed me onto my back, spreading his body over mine with a huge grin on his face. "What you tryna say?"

"I'm saying you need to stop talking and get to work."

"Baby, you ain't got to tell me twice."

~The end~

For information on post-abortion healing and emotional recovery, visit:

http://hopeafterabortion.com/

About the Author:

Married at sixteen, a mother twice by seventeen, and thrice a mother and divorced by twenty-four, Adrienne Thompson is no stranger to adversity. Not your typical teenage mother, she went on to complete her college degree and to earn her nursing license. She attributes God's faithfulness as the catalyst for her success in life. Now, having raised three children as a divorced mother, she is sharing a long-hidden talent and passion with the world. Using the lessons that life has so expertly taught her as a guideline (betrayal, abusive relationships, self-esteem issues, witnessing the deteriorating effects of drug abuse), she has created stories that will both entertain and inspire the reader. Adrienne currently resides in Arkansas in her newly empty nest. Formerly an RN, she now writes and publishes her stories full time. She is also a motivational speaker. Breathe Again is her 27th published work.

For more information about Adrienne Thompson and her books, visit:
http://adriennethompsonwrites.webs.com

Sign up for Adrienne's newsletter here: **http://eepurl.com/jnDmH**

Follow Adrienne on Twitter!
https://twitter.com/A_H_Thompson

Like Adrienne on Facebook!
https://www.facebook.com/AdrienneThompsonWrites

Join Adrienne's Facebook group!!

https://www.facebook.com/groups/674088779363625/

Follow Adrienne on Pinterest!

http://www.pinterest.com/ahthompsn/

Connect with Adrienne on Goodreads!

https://www.goodreads.com/author/show/5051327.Adrienne_Thompson

Be sure to check out these other titles by Adrienne Thompson:

The *Bluesday* Series:
Bluesday
Lovely Blues
Blues In The Key Of B
Locked out of Heaven (Tomeka's Story – A Bluesday Continuation)

The *Been So Long* Series:
Rapture (A Been So Long Prequel)
If (Wasif's Story) A Been So Long Prequel
Been So Long
Little Sister (Cleo's Story—a companion novel to Been So Long)
Been So Long 2 (Body and Soul)
Been So Long III (Whatever It Takes)
SEPTEMBER (The Christina Dandridge Story—a Been So Long companion novel)
Been So Long IV (Rhythm of Love)

The *Your Love Is King* Series:
Your Love Is King
Better

The *Ain't Nobody* Series:
Sedução (Seduction)—an Ain't Nobody Prequel
Ain't Nobody

The Latter Rain Series:
After the Pain
No Pain, No Gain
Joy and Pain

The *See Me* Series
See Me
See Me, Too

Stand-alone novels:
Home
When You've Been Blessed (Feels Like Heaven)
Summertime (A Novella)
Breathe Again

Fiction Anthology:
The Ex Chronicles – as a contributor

Nonfiction Titles:
Just Between Us (Inspiring Stories by Women) –as a contributor
Seven Days of Change (A Flash Devotional)

Poetry:
Poetry from the Soul… for the Soul, Volume II

All books are available at **amazon.com** and **barnesandnoble.com**.

Made in the USA
San Bernardino, CA
27 July 2018